SARASWATI SAMMAN WINNER

DUST ON PLANTS

(A Novel)

SARASWATI SAMMAN WINNER

DUST ON PLANTS

(A Novel)

Translated from Hindi by the Author

Govind Mishra

Ocean Books Pvt. Ltd.

ISO 9001:2015 Publishers

Published by
Ocean Books (P) Ltd.
4/19 Asaf Ali Road,
New Delhi-110 002 (INDIA)
e-mail: info@oceanbooks.in

ISBN 978-81-8430-493-0
DUST ON PLANTS
Novel by Govind Mishra

Edition
2025

Price
₹ 400.00 (Rupees Four Hundred only)

Printed at
R-Tech Offset Printers, Delhi

Dedicated to the
sweet memories of my dear friend
Amitabh Pandey

Dedicated to the

memory of my father

Amitabh Pandey

Who are you... What are you?

Exclude the early years of education and preparation and hold on to what you earned in the later years. This is what you are – it can be assumed, nay that is what is usually assumed. People know you for that only. You too. What, however, should have happened instead is just the opposite. You should have been known for what you were in the early years, when you had still not been corrupted by worldliness, when your essence was intact... had not evaporated. The later years... you should have yourself thrown out as soon as they ended, so that the original you, your real self could live on. In the later years, we are busy building for ourselves a reputation—may be through promotions from one position to another or by amassing wealth or via planned projection of our character, gentlemanliness, humaneness, etc. Now, what are you at this point of time? You are a post—Director of a prestigious institution of Social Studies. People know you only as Director. As prestige these days requires something extra, you became a social worker too. To show off that you are more than the post you occupy, you got associated with reputed institutions of social work. Maybe there was also little urge in you to do social work but the real motivation came from the latent lust for fame. In short, you failed to be yourself, became a lump of respectability instead. Not a human being, but a portrait which looks to viewers the way you want it to look. Overall, the portrait is of a famous intellectual—respectable, cultured, noble, of a good family, well off...also attractive to look at. Picture of a complete man. You can focus or project whatever side you so desire and whenever. The arrangement that, at a given time, you are seen the way you like to be seen is not visible either. This respectable personality has become your identity so naturally and completely that you never feel the necessity to pierce the facade and peep inside. Occasions do arise however, when a small crack appears. You see it. Now you may explore the crack or overlooking it remain, as always, complacent...., satisfied that you are viewed by people as you want to....

A department of the university invited you to address the students there. Two girl students came with the invitation. You could guess that the audience there would be small; you felt irritated—you are too reputed to address such small gatherings, only big inaugurations and chairing big seminars befit you! So, you pretended to be busy on that date and dismissed the girls. To keep up appearances, you suggested couple of alternative names. Now see, lies like these are as much part of your being as your reputation, which you cherish. But pray, the reputation which you feel you have—is it really accepted by the people at large or is it sycophancy, which your chosen few offer you in big spoons. Do you mean that people, who see you in poor light or think correctly about you, do not simply exist? Is there some such thing as your correct assessment? If so, what is it? If your identity is this reputation only, then how much of it has been really earned by you and how much engineered by you through publicity?

You can also be questioned about your social work. Is it really worth all the big words you use to describe it? You may confidently put forth the number and even weight of the books written by you, but what about their quality and the honesty of your thinking there? After sincere introspection, you would definitely conclude that very little is original there; largely it is words... words only.

Have you really devoted substantial part of your life to social work? Did you really give your best there or was it only a pastime? It was encashed by you twice – first as an addition to your reputation and, second time, as writing material for your books. You were all the time publicising the facade – that you were an activist, striving to change the society.... worse still that you seriously saw yourself in that role – height of self-deception! Did you really feel the pain of the wrongs being perpetrated on the common folk? Was it not simply a sham every time, so as to add a new feather to your cap?

Granted for a moment that this reputation of yours was not on account of publicity but just got built up around you incidentally, but partner! the fact remains that you always carry and project this self-image, enjoy doing it, knowing fully well that it is not what you really are. You hold on to this image even during introspections because it is convenient. Casting it away involves effort; it will also be painful for it will unfold your inner chaos, which you don't want to face.

So, with this appearance... pose, you carry on. You are fortunate that any such person who would tear off the cover with a knife, as it were, never entered your life. How unfortunate that despite all your intelligence, you would leave the world without even seeing yourself truthfully. The mirror was never placed before you.

You may complain that this sort of assessment doesn't do justice to you but the fact remains that people know you from things which you have achieved with the help of your image. This big house in a country where many do not have even a roof over their heads, this lawn, the iron-gate, car parked in the portico... these things give an idea about your bank balance, the locker which you will definitely be having, properties here and elsewhere. The girls who just left were seeing with wide-open eyes these things only, from which they assumed the important positions you held, your fame and wealth. They may be senior students of sociology but rest assured, they have not read a single line of yours, nor do they know about any of your social works, never heard you... but they did sense that you are a big man. Everyone feels that. This bunglow alone would make that impression. It overawed those girls and they immediately accepted that you are indeed what you are pronounced outside – intellectual of high class, reputed social worker. When you declined their invitation, you further raised your stature a few notches up... but did it go up in your self-estimate also? Sorry, no... and this realisation lagged behind painfully crawling inside you. From the verandah, you watched the girls go out, heard the sound of the iron-gate closing and were overall happy that you declined their invitation.

"Sir, I am doing M. Phil in Sociology. May I sit?"

"Please..."

Prem Prakash was on his study table. She sat down on the sofa before him. Her slim figure of medium height was covered with winter-clothing. Rather aged to be a student, she nevertheless looked one. Light fair complexion, ordinary features – neither sharp, nor dull. Scarf on bob-cut thick hair. Red lipstick. Complexion of the face was further subdued thanks to the winter wind and the facial cream. Prem Prakash noticed that her hands looked fairer than her face. She was ordinarily attractive... if you looked at her, you might not have the urge to continue looking but the gaze did not deflect either.

"Sir, I have come to invite you for delivering a lecture in our department."

"Two girls came yesterday and I told them that I won't be able to come."

"I know... yet I have come."

"Why?"

"Because all of us are eager to hear you. We will keep it on whatever date suits you... but come you must Sir!"

Prem Prakash could see the light glow that emanated from her face... self-confidence, albeit suppressed. The girl knew that nothing was special about her – neither she herself, nor her subject, nor department... and yet...

"But, why?"

"Because I have promised my Head that I would convince you... whatever way and you will agree."

"Wow! so interesting that you have already said 'yes' on my behalf."

"Sir! all of us desire that you kindly address us."

"But pray, why?"

"Because we are keen to hear you – otherwise also you should once a while come in the midst of students. How shall they be enlightened if people like you keep away?"

"You people do not read anything outside your curriculum, don't want to. Eagerness... thirst... all eyewash! College lectures, keynotes on the textbooks, you feel, are sufficient for you."

"Sir, you are right. Most of us are what you say, but there might be a few who because of their circumstances are not able to read anything outside their curriculum. Attending the university is no mean achievement for them. If only you knew about their circumstances..."

"Well, what's the use of being in the midst of those who won't understand me at all?" Prem Prakash, an eminent sociologist, was stuck.

"If even one out of them caught a single point made by you... he or she got enlightened to that extent. You should go for his or her sake."

"But where is that guy?"

"How do I know. May be there, may not be..."

"You mean, for the sake of one individual, who may be there, may not be... most probably will not be – for his or her sake, I should go to all sorts of places, even to such small gatherings?"

"Yes, because, as you said, everyone does not read what you have written."

"Those among you who are curious would eventually find out my books, read them today or tomorrow. If not you, your teachers will. And if even they do not, I don't care."

"But those who do not read or are not able to... how do you spread your message among them? If, towards that end, you have to resort to lecturing, what is wrong about it?"

"Things that matter to me are – one, writing what I have to; second, social work. Wandering here and there to lecture is a waste of time." Prem Prakash was really irritated.

"Sir, part of your writing, your thinking, your work would definitely come out in your speech. Your personality would speak... Besides, you are there before the people...."

Prem Prakash became thoughtful. It is true that our thoughts, ideas, deeds first cast their impression on ourselves and thus become essential part of our personality. People have indeed said about him—'Sir, vibrations flow from your personality.' There was some sense in what this ordinary almost uneducated woman-like girl was saying.

"O.K. if you people are determined, I shall come. Fifth, at three p.m. Not in the morning. That time is exclusively for my writing. I don't let anyone encroach upon it."

"Thank you, Sir! It's fine with us."

"Check up with your Head, suits him or not."

"Sir, I shall ensure that it suits him."

"How?"

"As I brought you round."

Prem Prakash laughed, she too after him. The atmosphere turned pleasant... but for a few seconds only because just then Prem Prakash got up.

"Let someone come to escort," he said with a stiff countenance.

"Sir! the department has not been provided with a car, nor do they have money to bear taxi charges. I will come with my vehicle; you be my pillion ride."

She pointed towards her scooty, parked outside.

Prem Prakash who was heading towards the inner door suddenly stopped. Lips sealed, he threw a glance towards the scooty and was now staring hard at her. What does she think of him? He agreed to address an audience below average, no demand of any honorarium and now is asked to be a pillion ride! What would people think? The idea of travelling on a scooter scared him. Never in his life did he ride this stuff. In student days, it was a bicycle, later he took to car straightaway.

"Sir!..." she looked in askance. Prem Prakash collected himself and said haltingly.

"I am very scared of sitting on a scooter."

"Really..."

Laughter trickled out like a stream from her. "You are scared of sitting on a scooter.... really...?"

She was laughing, while speaking. A symphony it was... her laughter.

She went on laughing. When the laughter finally stopped, she said with a grave countenance.

"You are a kid... out and out. Don't worry, I am there." That moment she had become older than her age.

"I sat on a scooter only once or twice in my life." Prem Prakash confessed.

"I thought social workers have experience of everything associated with the common man."

That is how it should be... Prem Prakash found himself cornered. Once while bathing in the sea, he had also laughed like this at his poet-friend, who was very scared of entering the sea. From the shore, he enviously watched Prem Prakash playing with the waves. 'What would you know of the sea, unless you felt the sea-waves dashing against you.' Prem Prakash had then told his friend, who had written quite a few poems on sea and rated them as some of his best.

"Your car... you drive it?" She asked, pointing towards the car parked in the portico.

"Yes."

"You can drive a four-wheeler but are scared of a two-wheeler!"

She started laughing again. Outside, a branch of a mango-tree laden with new leaves gently stirred.

"All right, you come but we shall go in my car."

"Thank you, Sir. I shall come on 5th at quarter to 3 p.m. Shall also remind you on telephone in the morning."

"All right."

She would now come to Prem Prakash's house every third or fourth day. Friendly with his wife and mother soon enough, she would sit and converse with them leisurely. While coming or going back, she would not forget peeping into Prem Prakash's study and wishing him. So long she was there, the house was resonant with zestful sounds. To the house where otherwise three elderly people moved sluggishly and the general atmosphere for that reason was stale and dull... even morbid, she, as it were, brought mornings in her bag, scattered its warmth all around. She was brief with Prem Prakash, whose time, she thought, was very precious – he might be engaged with some high thinking, big writing. Little did she know that while she was there, she was the centre of attention for him.

That day in the Department, the welcome speech was delivered by her, thanks-giving too. In the midst of students and teachers, she shone like a candle in a dark room. She accompanied Prem Prakash on return. While driving when Prem Prakash's grip was on the gear... her palm from nowhere came and sat on Prem Prakash's hand as his was on the gear. It lay there for a while. Before Prem Prakash could feel something, she withdrew.

What does that mean... I kept thinking. Each action of ours – does it invariably have some meaning? Do instinctive actions, which originate from the subconscious always have some meaning? Most probably, on her part, it was an innocent act—small and spontaneous, devoid of any meaning. At the most, it was a gesture of gratitude—that on her request, I went to address them, after all. Had it been anything else, it would have registered in me likewise...then and there.

With new leaves on trees all around, the atmosphere in the University-campus was exuberant. Weather was getting out of the clutches of winter. Kutruk squeaked intermittently from somewhere, announcing the imminent change in the weather. Prem Prakash felt like having a stroll with her in the campus, sitting with her on some lonely bench in the fast-approaching dusk, reliving the days, when he studied in the university.

He controlled himself. What would she think... and they who saw them – an elderly person of Professor's age sitting in a romantic posture with a girl student, half his age?

One day I saw her fair arms come out of the red shawl, which covered them. So smooth, delicate, evenly carved out! Sensitivity, like gentle wind, blew from them. Noticing that I was lost looking at her arms, she immediately pulled them back in the shawl. She was slightly disturbed, appeared to be little angry over the way I was looking. Her face however, was blank... and she took the arms back mechanically. She must have, however, noticed that my gaze was different this time, so far I hadn't looked at her that way. To be honest, I didn't plan

anything. The beautiful arms... just came out, caught my gaze and I kept looking till she covered them again.

Today, while she was going back, I came to see her off, up to her scooty parked on the roadside. As she sat on the scooty, her salwar moved up slightly and the toe over the sandle was exposed for a second – very fair, reddish, round – that the salwar came down and covered it again.

Peaks of Kanchanjanga peep out like this suddenly for a second, only to hide themselves again in the clouds.

The special tinge of a woman's personality is reflected by some particular part of her body or some particular posture of hers. I was not attracted by the beautiful eyes of this lady or her charming figure. Why only the arms and the toe? What do they convey?

She is married. She invited Prem Prakash and his wife to her house. Prem Prakash immediately agreed. No ifs and buts this time.

Her house.

Mother-in-law, a wounded tigress. Angry look all the time. Even a newcomer is looked by her with contempt and pouncing eyes. Looks as if the whole world had wronged her. She could not avenge herself but was constantly on the lookout. Her face never softens, no shadow of any love ever appears there. While enquiring about her health, Prem Prakash happened to ask about the particular ailment she suffered from. Down came a cynical response – 'your question itself is wrong. You should have asked – what is the ailment which is not there!' She is nonetheless a patient of blood pressure and diabetes – which every third person these days is. She is slim but not emaciated like a patient. Always angry, it is her mind that is diseased. A satisfied person is always in a blissful disposition, which his face reflects and which carries even a disproportionate body amiably. This lady's body is proportionate but her mind is dishevelled... so even her body provokes contempt. Even her slim figure is a load she has to carry. She feels that the entire world has been tormenting her since God knows when. She tries not to think about her physical ailments at all, but... she does only those household chores which do not require much of a finesse, e.g. cleaning wheat/rice, etc., washing clothes, sweeping, dusting also, if the maid doesn't turn up. She doesn't cook, ironing never... hundred percent chance of getting burnt there! She is not entrusted with chores where forgetfulness can lead to mishaps or where a certain level of efficiency is required. This has led to further erosion of her self-confidence and consequent bitterness. She spends most of her time doing ordinary chores, cursing her fate. In between, if someone came her way, she would so scold, abuse or taunt him that the fellow would not forget for days.

Her routine is not time-bound. She may not bathe till 3 p.m., depending which chore drags on. Similarly, she has no fixed time for lunch or dinner. Everyone in the house takes lunch separately as per his/her convenience. They do try, however, to dine together. If she is free, then she may come to the dining table, but no one waits for her. They avoid her in fact – she can utter anything... something foul also. No one, however, dare suggest that she may dine later. For formality's sake, she is requested alright... but only once. If she doesn't turn up, everyone heaves a sigh of relief. She carries on... floating on the waves of her mumblings. No one disturbs her. A point, however, comes, when her self-pity is too much for her. Then she takes to quarrelling – mostly with her husband, frequently with her daughter-in-law and sometimes with her son too. With the son, however, it is always a subdued affair. Not that she loves him, she is scared that she may lose him.

Husband of such a woman—the girl's father-in-law – is what he would be. Old before his age. If his wife floats in timelessness, he keeps himself bound by hours and minutes. Get up at four, take the dog out to ease. Toilet and bathe on return. An hour thereafter for pooja. During that pious hour, complete silence – 'maunvrit', even shadow of any human being should not fall upon him. Otherwise also he doesn't speak much. When wife be cruel – cruelty stamped on her face, hot wind blowing out of her nostrils all the time – there is no alternative anyway. His wife holds him squarely responsible for her ruined life. Was only a clerk in an insignificant department, lacked even the intelligence of doing his job, not to talk of making underhand money. She somehow managed the house with his meagre salary. Now after his retirement, she a mother-in-law, is reduced to be a maid-servant. She leaves no occasion to throw at her husband a severe look or a taunt – see this is what you have made of me! He avoids coming her way, as far as possible. Luckily, the house is two-storeyed and his room is on the ground floor, hers on the first. As a matter of penance, he tries to do even the chores she should be doing, e.g. cooking in the evening. His life, however, revolves around the dog. The dog gave him what his wife could not – love and no reproach. He takes it out morning and evening. Day time he keeps himself occupied with all sorts of things – worshipping, hearing discourses on T.V., reading scriptures, kitchen work, going to the market, etc. Takes more and more work on himself. All the while, however, he is focussed on the dog. Does not leave himself unoccupied even for a minute; yet he feels his wife's eyes are piercing into his back all the time. Running away from them, he tries to remain busy, calm and satisfied. That way he has kept himself largely free from disease. Speaks only that much which is required, is not very keen on sitting with any visitor, because, at that time, his wife's gaze pounces upon him straight.

The progeny of a disease-free man and a diseased woman is the girl's husband.

Father managed a diploma for him on the strength of which he got a job in a private firm. Simultaneously, from an institution of dubious name, he procured the degree of what was called 'Jyotishacharya'. Back from the office, he throws away his pant-shirt – a burden he carried all the day long. Now attired in dark red long kurta and lungi, yellow sandal pasted on the forehead, big bead garlands round the neck and wrists, he heads towards the outer room of the house, converted into a temple. On a big throne here stands a huge statue of the Goddess Kali – with smaller statues on its lower steps. Along with them on the right side is kept a mounted photograph of his guru and in the same position on the left side, a similar photo of himself. Just beside the celestial throne is placed a one-seater sofa. This is the gaddi... on which he sits, the young guru. Any visitor any time... he would rush to the temple, place himself on the gaddi and grant audience there.

When the girl introduced Prem Prakash and his wife to her in-laws, she was present, participated in the conversation also but for meeting her husband, she pushed them to the temple side and quietly withdrew.

In the temple, it was dark red all the way – dress of the Goddess, her tongue, dress of the young guru, the sofa turned gaddi, the steel-plate containing pieces of gram, peanuts and ilaychidana, the carpet... all dark red, irritating to the eyes. Her husband was seated on the sofa in the posture of a Mahant (religious teacher). Not even a chair around, Prem Prakash and his wife had perforce to sit on the floor, almost at the feet of the young guru. The arrangement was such that the visitors would either keep standing or sit on the carpet. That way the young guru would make every visitor sit below him, however senior he or she be in age, education or wealth. Himself seated on his gaddi, he would intermittently go on looking at the heavy kara (a thick anklet-like ornament of silver) which he had put on his right foot. Thus, he would make the visitors notice it. The kara was proof of Deeksha taken by him from the Guru, whose photo adorned the celestial throne. The house was constructed by his father, but the nameplate outside, was of the young guru – his name prefixed by 'Swami' and suffixed by 'Anand'. Morning and evening Aarti, open for all, was performed either by the young guru or his father. At night, the young guru, seated on his gaddi, would listen to the problems of the visitors, suggest ways of solving them, read their horoscopes, tell about their future – a thing everyone is curious about. That apart, the young guru would come to the temple and be seated on his gaddi any time any visitor turned up. He was a modern swami, carried a mobile in place of a 'sumirni mala' (beads – garland used for counting mantras chanted). On his fleshy fingers, he had rings studded with precious stones.

The young guru kept short hair, so that his forehead, yellow sandal pasted on it, was prominent. His face was like a big rasgullah (a round sweet) cracked from a side. Thick lips, fluffy fingers. Prem Prakash felt that young guru's appearance was as coarse and dull as his wife's was sensitive and sharp. Mixture of technical education and religion, he could not attain a grade in either, lost the essence of both. The young guru expected that the visitors would put questions to him with reverence and there is no dearth of them if Indian women are around.

Prem Prakash and his wife bowed before the Goddess, put Rs. 51 on the celestial throne and sat down. Mrs. Prem Prakash was anxious to know about the future of her son, who was serving faraway in the south. She gave the boy's horoscope to the young guru, who appeared to study it for a while. Thereafter, he counted something on the pores of his fingers – forwards and backwards. Finally, he closed his eyes in reflection, slipped into Dhyan-mudra. After a while, he opened his eyes and said, "Detailed reading of the horoscope can be prepared in writing and sent in due course. Presently, however, some general things can be told. The horoscope is good. Health of the boy is good. His parents are good, he would always keep getting something or the other from them.

Great readings indeed! Prem Prakash laughed in his sleeves. If the horoscope is of a young boy, his health is bound to be good. If you know that the boy's parents are well-to-do, you can conveniently predict that the boy shall continue receiving from them. Detailed reading later on... means you can always get it prepared from outside. Mrs. Prem Prakash was listening with awe and reverence. These swamis flourish because of such ladies! Out of mischief, Prem Prakash asked –

"How many marriages of the boy are indicated?"

Searching something in the horoscope, the young guru answered –

"Why, one only. The marital life is good."

Prem Prakash winked at his wife – that she could see the knowledge of astrology of the man revered by her. In reality, first marriage of the boy had thrown up lots of disputes and quarrels between the couple, eventually leading to the break-up. The second marriage was solemnised only a few months back. The parents were anxious because the boy was short-tempered. Mrs. Prem Prakash was, however, not to be disheartened. She had put forth her own horoscope in the meantime and was keen to know her future.

Prem Prakash kept mum, while the two conversed. The big photograph of the young guru, placed honourably in the midst of gods, was attracting his attention repeatedly. Seated with the Gods! The fellow has already turned himself into a God, even though alive!! A chain of thoughts ensued – how can one be a guru without knowledge, deep study of scriptures is a must. Had the young guru studied the Indian scriptures, the concept of suppressing, even erasing one's ego – which is very basic – would have surely dawned on him and then he would not have kept his photograph with the deities. The professional learning of the young-guru – whatever it was – would consist of informations only, any knowledge was faraway. The young guru feels elated sitting on this gaddi, repeatedly glancing at the kara – indicate that the man is terribly hungry for recognition, which he couldn't hope for in his job... although work at whatever level, if done well, does bring acclaim and recognition. That was a far-fetched proposition. Here was a short-cut. Maybe he wants to create another source of income through astrology and associated activities, e.g. making horoscopes, their readings, suggesting ways to ward off evil, fasts to be observed, precious stones to be worn, getting the genuine ones for the customers, etc. Offerings in the temple were there in any case. Considering that so many were already there in this occupation, substantial earnings were ruled out. Thirst for recognition appeared to be young guru's primary motivation.

"Won't you ask something about your future?" Done with Mrs. Prem Prakash, the young guru turned towards Prem Prakash.

"My future? The position one could aspire in my official life, I have attained. Family – done. Now only the past is there, no future..."

"Hope is life, one should not give it up until the last breath."

"Majority of us live, because we don't die. We go on like machines... aging simultaneously. Nothing worthwhile happens in our lives... but we live on...

"Life is eternally on the move."

While the young guru was throwing one cliche after another, Prem Prakash was getting more and more introspective. What really can now happen in his life? Nothing. Few more books, a couple of awards, maybe one more post of little higher recognition... What else? Guru kept going, however.

"People around you – your parents, wife, children. It is but natural to be concerned about them. You may ask about their future."

"Father is no more. Mother is eighty-one. Her future is that she would drag on, her health continuously falling. Wife – her inclination towards children will increase, she would develop arthritis; bickerings with husband would increase, what else! She has two children. You have already told about one, about the other she would ask next time."

Foretelling the future of his family laughingly, Prem Prakash got up. Had he not done so, his wife would have lingered on.

The young guru with his fluffy fingers picked up from the red plate below few pieces of grams and peanuts and by turns dropped them in their hands from a distance. The 'prasad' smelt perspiration of young guru's palm. Prem Prakash, couldn't put it in his mouth, nor could he decide what to do with it.

"Keep coming," the young guru said.

Prem Prakash didn't reply. His wife did. "One gets peace in the temple. Meeting people like you increases knowledge."

"Exactly!"

That word... the young guru used repeatedly. Its meaning, the tone in which it was uttered, amply indicated the self-satisfaction which he carried inside. It was not equanimity in happiness and grief nor distancing from the world – which the scriptures taught. It was also not ego satisfaction as normally understood. A mediocre, who was neither knowledgeable nor a good conversationalist, was taking advantage of the idleness of Indians – who would bow before all the temples falling on the way, bow ten times before the temple they pass by ten times a day. It was so easy to be a swami or guru of them. That he did not have knowledge or any spiritual experience never occurred to the young guru. He felt elated amidst people in obeisance. The oft-spoken, oft-heard things... trash which he uttered, were mistaken by him to be pieces of knowledge. Uttering them, he felt to be on top of the world. Prem Prakash thought – young guru may not be great, things uttered may also not be so but the fact that both were recognised as such by the people around him made the difference. It was an achievement for a person, who otherwise was a cypher, to become a swami – the short cut didn't matter. Even though average, the young guru did not wish to remain so. Ironically, he took an ordinary way to become something special. He would put up only one disposition – smilingly looking at people who came, softly speaking to them... as if, all the time, he was saying only one thing unto them – "everything is fine with you and so with me."

While returning, Prem Prakash was surprised at the contempt for the young guru... that grew in him so fast.

How could she be living with these creatures... she, the daughter-in-law, the girl, so sensitive and sharp?

Although her research work was not directly related to the area of which Prem Prakash was a specialist, yet it touched the broader contours of sociology and Prem Prakash was a famous sociologist. Her dissertation would certainly get weight, if an interview of Prem Prakash got incorporated there. So, after taking an appointment, she interviewed him in his study. By the time they finished, she had become quite frank with him. Most of her questions were elementary and academic, yet Prem Prakash didn't get irritated as he was prone to do. He answered patiently. Now the stray points arising from the interview were being informally discussed. The initial hesitation that she was talking to an eminent scholar, alone in his study, had disappeared long back. Right now she felt exhilarated.

"Sir! Is any path in life so perfect that the moment you take to another, the feeling of having gone astray would overtake you?"

"For getting an answer to this sort of question, you will have to approach a saint. There is one in your house already."

Prem Prakash laughed but she became grave, as if someone had cut a dirty joke on her. Her fair complexion turned blackish. A thin strip of her shining hair came down on her face, dividing it into two. Her eyes became so sad that Prem Prakash got alarmed.

"I mean... saints have been grappling with such a question since time immemorial. I am an ordinary man after all."

She didn't say anything. Prem Prakash's earlier remark had touched her deep and she was stuck there.

"I was just joking. In fact, your husband or I are not even qualified to grapple with this issue. The path in question can be found by someone only for himself, that too, if his or her consciousness rises to that level. Usually, it does not... then what's the use of putting on the cloak of sainthood."

The explanation relaxed her a little and she could come out.

"You can certainly answer, if you care to."

"Do you think my consciousness has touched that height?"

"Honesty is more important. What you spoke in the Department, you speak in your house too and what little I know, you do the same, live the same. This honesty is a bigger thing than the heightened consciousness you associate with religious people."

"Mercy please! Don't blow me like a balloon, Prem Prakash laughed, "I know, I have numerous human weaknesses and I don't very much try to get rid of them. I am happy to be human."

"That's all right... but you must have given a thought to this issue sometime or the other. I think you are just avoiding because I don't deserve, I am not that intelligent."

"That is not correct. Who could be more deserving than you? You are of the new generation, intelligent and curious... but I don't know what should I say because I couldn't discover such a path for myself, didn't try probably."

"OK... leave it. Tell me—there is a path, which the society hands over to you, sort of puts up before you to take. Now does this path have such sanctity that the moment you take to another, you start feeling that you are going astray."

"Mostly it is so... because the social order looms large and heavy. Of course, there is always a second path... but following it is looked down upon as waywardness, even madness. Only a few who have enormous confidence in themselves are able to traverse it. Majority are caught in the conflict – the path sanctioned by the society or the one they would like to tread."

"Which one is right?"

"What is right or wrong is never easy to say. This much can, however, be said that while no struggle is involved in following the socially sanctioned path, when you take to the self-created one, you are in for difficulties. There are thorns all the way."

"And that's why, majority follow the socially sanctioned."

"Yes."

"Which path did you take?"

"I feel I didn't take either. I just continued rolling over whatever path came my way. In fact, the creature known as the intellectual is a big coward, an escapist. I continued hiding behind books. Sometimes, I did some analysis, established a few norms, carved out certain principles, projected as thesis an idea or a combination of ideas flowing out of them but immediately felt that I was lying. By making such propositions, we only confuse those who otherwise are comfortable leading their lives away from biggish thoughts, enjoying day-to-day things, with the naive belief that those things alone matter."

Could I have said this outside – what, so unhesitatingly I told her? Before her, it is so very difficult not to speak the truth, She goads you to face yourself. The truth inside perforce comes out.

"You mean – knowledge is useless."

"I won't say that... but often have I seen an uneducated person living his life much better. The more a man becomes knowledgeable, the more he gets entangled in the cobweb of intelligence, whereas the uneducated gets along freely."

"It is so because he blindly follows the way set by the society – as the bullocks carry on the cart mechanically on the trodden path."

"Yes, majority do just that. Some, in order to delude themselves that they are on their individual path, create some small diversion such as mine – social service, reading, writing etc., but their central path or main line remains the one set by the society."

"The path carved out by us for ourselves, moving on it as we wish – that would look waywardness?"

"Certainly, and most certainly, if it doesn't, at least keep cover of the socially sanctioned."

"Even the educated like you would think so?"

"A few may keep in view the context of the individual whose life it is anyway. They may approve... but majority of the educated also go by social acceptability."

"What's then the use of their being educated?"

"Education is relevant only when you are operating in the area of your profession. When it comes to the basics of life, what is expected of the uneducated is expected of the educated also – accept the socially sanctioned."

"People like you... can't you change it?"

Prem Prakash was silenced. He was looking at her – the girl could think, was sharp whereas his own thought-process, after a point started drifting towards the area, which stored all the good things being talked about since time immemorial. He couldn't keep original or remain honest, whereas this girl could... and for quite a distance.

"Did you ever oppose?" she further asked.

"We may feel and express love, hate, attachment, jealousy, anger, sadness, indifference, kindness, etc. in an individual way, may let ourselves go while living these emotions... transcend or sublimate them to an extent... but what is socially acceptable or not can't be changed easily."

"How can we feel that we are indeed living and not simply existing? What gives that feeling?"

"It would vary from individual to individual."

"What is it for you, achievements?"

"Achievements do not very much attract me. Any work done for some reward cannot give the feeling you are talking about. One achievement goads for the second, second to the third one, and so on; we are running all the time, panting! Is it living really? The feeling that we are indeed living can come only from a work, which is its own reward... for example, prayer, if it is an end in itself and is not aimed to attain salvation, not even peace. In everyone's life, there are such calamities before which all his achievements, distinctions, etc. pale into insignificance. Therefore, talking of achievements in life or achievements in terms of some work, etc. is sheer foolishness."

"Work for its own sake is the privilege of those who have a relaxed life. People whose life is a continuous struggle for making both ends meet... where would they find their raison d'etre?"

"Probably, in their struggle itself. You appear to be correct when you say that questions pertaining to meaning, substance or essence or life arise only where there is no physical struggle for living. For others, where is the time? Sometimes I feel, thinking itself is a luxury."

"No, everyone sometime or the other pauses to reflect on his life. Standards of thinking may vary. But even an ordinary fellow in the midst of his day-to-day struggle of life pauses and reflects – what he is, what his life is, what he was, what he can be, etc. It's another matter that he is not very original or coherent, and much before reaching somewhere, gets relieved by surrendering himself to God.

"What... what do you think about your life?" Prem Prakash interrupted.

"Only they can think, who are at least sure that their life is theirs after all. My life is not mine any way. See, if it was not the pleasure of my husband, I could not have studied. Is it in my hands as to how many children would I bear? Nothing is in my hands!"

"You mean, the situation an Indian woman finds herself in?"

"No, many Indian women have gone far ahead. I mean my life."

Shadow of deep sadness fell over her face. She couldn't speak further, her throat got probably choked.

She appeared to be looking beyond – easy chair on which sat Prem Prakash, verandah and the house-boundary further... still further the rugged road, which had not been done for years.

It was the beginning of the rainy season. Dark clouds were gathering in the sky. First, there was a thin shower, the fragrance of the wet earth started playing at the nostrils. Following came the wind, eager to assimilate the fragrance and scatter it all over. Evening time, rainy clouds above... under their shadow, her face had further darkened. Like a statue she sat looking outwards as though sleeping... her eyes wide open, of course.

Darkness was setting in. Heavy rains appeared to be imminent. Even as she was continuously looking straight, she woke up, as it were – she must leave. Started collecting her things, preparing to move. Just as she was getting up, it started raining.

These were not the clouds which would rain a little and disappear, nor were they peculiar clouds of a city, now raining here and immediately moving on to another part. This rain was going to stay. While it moved in its pace, she followed her own. Leisurely, she came out of the room, stepped into her sandals lying in the verandah and started moving out... as if it was not raining at all. She also forgot to go inside to say good-bye to Prem Prakash's wife and mother – as she always did.

"Aye... listen, how would you go... it is raining. Wait awhile." Prem Prakash almost shouted from behind.

"It's o.k." she said coldly without turning.

"You will get drenched. Wait for a while. It may stop raining."

"It won't."

"How do you know?"

"Because it is I who have to go."

"Bravo! means that the entire Nature is against you. Have you got a rain-coat?"

"No."

"All right, now listen. Park your scooty here in the portico. I would take you home in my car. You can come tomorrow morning to collect the scooty.

She didn't say anything.

For little safety from the rains, she put her dupatta on her head, brought the scooty inside and parked it in the portico, next to Prem Prakash's car. In the meantime, Prem Prakash had picked up the car-key, informed his mother and wife that he was going to drop her home. He took the car out. She followed and closed the gate behind it, in course got wet; she never hurried to save herself from rains. In the same slow pace, she came up to the car, and sat beside Prem Prakash... the same place, where she sat when she had escorted him to the Department and back.

It was not raining heavily but continuously alright. One could sense it from inside the car – the way rain-drops were falling on the bonnet.

She is quite careless, doesn't even keep the rain-coat. Had she gone in the scooty, she must have got drenched, could have fallen sick. Something happens to her all of a sudden. She was normal during the interview. The moment conversation came to her life, she went into a trance. She brought her scooty inside, opened and closed the gate, sat in the car, and all this while, she has been in trance. She is in it even now... and has been quiet throughout.

Having come some distance, Prem Prakash noted that the car was on a narrow lane, whereas it should have been on the main road. It was some inner lane – trees on one side, bungalows on the other, bungalows with distances in between. All around it was wet and lonely. When and how did they get into this little road... she didn't point out either. Prem Prakash stopped the car, looked around to locate. They were under the trees. The rain fell incessantly through the leaves of the trees, producing music on the car. The shower on the bulbs of the electricity poles appeared as though little insects, bent upon burning themselves, were hovering over the light. The sound of the rain was all around, intense on the trees above them.

"Appears we have lost the way. Darkness, rain over and above, can't see properly."

No response from her... as if she was not there at all.

Prem Prakash, who was looking around all this while, now looked at her. She was sitting on the car-seat exactly as she sat on the chair in Prem Prakash's study, a short while ago. Lifeless, vacant eyes looking in emptiness, colour of the face fading. There was desolation in her eyes as far as one could see – a long path barren and lonely.

Just then something glittered. Prem Prakash initially thought it was lightening, then he thought some plants were glittering in the darkness. Her fair and beautiful arms had come out of the kurta half way... arms – well-built, proportionate, round and so smooth that a finger, if placed on them, would slip down.

The hands were bright and speaking.

Taking her hand which was on his side, Prem Prakash kissed the palm; then, as if under delirium, went on kissing the full arm, rubbing his eyes on its smoothness repeatedly. While his lips were on the other side of the palm, he happened to see her eyes – they were as lifeless as before – caves... sad and desolate.

How big is this trance which from my study has come so far, she remaining the same. In this state only she brought her scooty in the portico. From that point to my kissing her full arm – she has been

looking at me with vacant eyes, doing the same even now. My infatuation... where did it come from? She could have flown into a rage. That would have been better than her looking at me vacantly like this.

"Drive on. Turn right, that is the way," taking her hand away, she said coldly. Her tone was a little tough.

One early morning, she called. Prem Prakash was busy in his study, and mother and wife in daily chores. Getting Prem Prakash on the line, she gave her name and immediately, as if the stone blocking it had been removed, the stream gushed out....

"What am I, will you please tell... a piece of paper which is rubbed repeatedly with a shoe, turning it into a cluster of holes... or a cub you run over by your car, speed away and never look back?"

Prem Prakash was aghast – was she rebuking him for his behavior that rainy evening?

"Am I a commodity or an animal and, if a wife, then not even a human being? My willingness or unwillingness is not worth a tuppence? The whole night he tore me into pieces, did not spare any part of my body, pulled my hair, forcibly took out my clothes, nailed my breasts, pressed his dirty teeth here and there, rubbed me repeatedly..."

Her voice, which in the beginning was hoarse, got choked here... and she started crying. However, she resumed immediately... same voice, heavy and hoarse, caught-up somewhere between anger and frustration.

"How insulting! Someone grinding you like this! Can you, after all this, still desire to live? He is a butcher, a hypocrite, would sit on the temple seat like a saint – with a face round as his belly; plump... fluffy face, oozing sweetness for outsiders. The same fellow under cover of night gets so cruel towards his wife! Tilak adorned on his forehead, he listens to people, suggests them ways to overcome their hardships and with his wife…? Is she of a different species, not human? The girl might not have been at all willing to marry you, but once the seven rounds by the fire are over, you are the master, you have all the rights! If you kill in one stroke, law might be after you… so kill her like this day by day, inch by inch. Kill her spirit… prerogative of the husband! I die each such night, detest each pore of my body, I hate to live... but shamelessly, next day, I get going again. He has all the rights, I have none... not even the right to desire or not… just because I am a woman. We two had got married but he alone has the right. Is there any right which I have? What do I live for… to be rubbed and murdered each day like this? Am I even alive… If yes, I curse it, I don't want to live...”

“Come... come!” Prem Prakash got frightened. “You should not think like that.”

“What like that”... she almost snubbed him... “he may behave like a carnivore and I am not allowed even to think against him? ‘He is after all my husband’ – I know this is all you would say....”

“No I mean... about not wanting to live. Don't think like that.”

“Why shouldn't I? Can you tell me one reason why I should live?”

“Yes, for your child.”

“I had no desire to be a mother. Parents of that man needed a toy to play with, to while away their time. What will my child be in this environment? What shall I be able to make him other than a pandit… the tribe I hate. Hypocrites – day time a sadhu, tilak painted on the forehead, at night a demon.”

“Listen… I agree… it is misbehaviour.”

"Misbehaviour? Either you don't know the correct word, which I don't believe is true in your case or you are deliberately condoning because you also happen to be a male."

"See... we will some day sit and talk about this at length.... only you and I. Relax right now. You can come whenever you feel like."

"I won't...."

And she hung up. The bitterness with which it was said left Prem Prakash shaken.

Probably, underneath this rage is also the ire which had come out only partially in her reaction to my behaviour that rainy evening – the way she pulled her arm away from my lips and dryly asked me to drive on. Did I care then for her willingness or otherwise? I went on passionately kissing her arm. She might not have said then in so many words but the ire was surely reflected in her eyes. It lay inside all this while, having come out only now, mixed with the anger for her husband. She must be thinking that basically my conduct was no different from that of her husband. Strange that the ire towards me had not subsided, and she shared such intimate things with me, of all the persons. What led her to communicate all this to me or there was no prior thinking? She just picked up the phone and started throwing out whatever lay inside her on whosoever was at the other end.

No, she could not tell such intimate things about her husband to any Tom, Dick and Harry.

Such a girl could commit suicide!

Should I call her? I don't have even her phone number, I was complacent that she would come over when she wants to, junior and a student as she is, though I was doubtful after my misbehaviour that rainy evening.

Looks like a wounded bird has come over the canopy of branches on my gate. Sitting there, it licks its wounds. When it flutters, blots of blood appear below the feathers. I step out to pick it up. Frightened it readies to fly away, even in that wounded stage. I come back. The bird continues to lick the wounds. While doing so, insecure, it looks here and there, towards me too.

What kind of a person is he... her husband! When he sits on his gaddi, he is sweet like a rasgolla for the stranger sitting opposite; the same person under cover of darkness is so cruel... with a being as intimate as his wife! Status. In one, the status is that of a guru, hence, compassion, kindness and the like. In the other, it is that of a husband – the Master. Hence, master-servant relationship bordering upon the cruel. It is the males who have spread the notion that women are masochists, happy with such cruel behaviour. The truth, however, appears to be otherwise.

'She won't come' she had said, but she came just a few days after. Prem Prakash was looking for the scars... of what she had talked about the other day. There was none however. She didn't even remember that despite little familiarity with Prem Prakash, she had shared such intimate things with him. Right then, she was a cheerful chirping bird. She was coming from the University. She carried with her a small box of sweets and her marksheet. Results of her M.Phil. exam had been declared – she got first division and second position in the University. Rather heading straight to Prem Prakash in his study, she reached the dining table via the back-door and gave the news first to Prem Prakash's mother, then to his wife, albeit a little loudly so that Prem Prakash in his room may also overhear. Immediately, the three inhabitants of the house gathered around the dining table.

She gave her marksheet to Prem Prakash. He put his specs on and started scanning it. His mother and wife congratulated her straightaway and helped themselves with pieces of sweets from the box which she had opened in the meantime. Then she put the box before Prem Prakash, who picked up a piece of sweet for himself. As he was going to put it in his mouth... his hand inadvertently took a turn towards her mouth. "Hearty congrats... such good marks even when you were looking after the household..."

Prem Prakash's hand carrying the sweet reached her mouth, which opened and closed as naturally after taking the sweet inside. Her face reddened a little, but embarrassment or anything of that sort was not there at all. As for Prem Prakash, he didn't know what was he doing. Mother and wife, however, looked at him with amazement. For them, it was unbecoming of Prem Prakash to act so intimate with a girl.

"Sir, I was first in the University, but have been taken down to the second position."

"How?"

"See the score. Only in the third paper it is low. This has been purposefully done. Examiner of this paper was not any outsider but my Head, Dr. Kaushik. He had told Karuna in advance that she would top."

"Is Karuna related to him?"

"No, she comes from a rich family and you ask anyone about our Head. He takes money."

"You didn't give."

"How could I? I am indebted to my husband that he sent me for studies at all. Wherefrom could I pay?

Prem Prakash looked at the marksheet again. The anomaly also struck him – a student scoring over seventy per cent in each paper gets stuck up at thirty-seven in the paper examined by Dr. Kaushik! She was right. He felt deep sympathy for her again – poor creature, must be feeling that injustice is done to her everywhere, home or outside.

"Doesn't matter. These marks are also no mean achievement."

"Marks is not the issue; it is that I shall not get the gold medal. I had topped in High School and gold medal was announced in my name. I was asked whether I would like to take gold medal or cash. On my behalf, my mother informed the school that I would prefer cash. I desired so much to go to the stage and take the Medal... instead money was sent home and was collected by my mother. I didn't get the gold medal then, nor would I get it now. I never get what I desire."

Her eyes got watery. As tears were about to trickle down, she took them on her dupatta. She was cheerful only a little earlier, sad soon after. The fresh face had shrunk. She was controlling herself, trying to appear brave. Changes come over her so quickly – Prem Prakash was thinking – or deep inside her, there is a rock of sadness. The rock for a while gets enveloped by a small cloud of some gaiety. The moment that cloud is blown away, the rock raises its head again, pressing her all the more. Her sadness disturbed Prem Prakash. He would have liked to clasp her, comfort her then and there, had she been alone with him. He tried to meet her eyes affectionately, also to see whether there was any remnant of the intimacy she had established that day by sharing with him the atrocities suffered at the hands of her husband. There was none.

They moved to the back courtyard, she following Prem Prakash's mother and wife. Prem Prakash came back to his room. He tried to overhear. Feminine exchanges. In between, he heard her murmuring – (in course of a sequence or just like that) 'in her house, there is parochial panditau atmosphere, which she doesn't like, she is compelled to partake in religious sittings, hours are wasted, studies suffer, she gets only four hours' sleep'.

Inside her, there is so much, itching to come out. She does not even ensure that she communicates with proper persons. How intimate is she with my mother and wife that she should be talking about her family matters with them? Since there is no one to share with, she communicates with whosever comes her way. Feels relieved. Right now, maybe she is not telling my mother and wife but me. She is in the courtyard and I in my study. The door of the study is open. She is sure that I would be listening. At times, she raises the pitch of her voice, as if telling me—Listen... Aye, you... who are not listening... you have to....

While returning, she peeped inside Prem Prakash's study. "Bye sir... I am going."

"Come here."

She came near the writing table. He whispered—"See me tomorrow at 4 p.m. in the lake park. At the gate... main gate... I shall be at the main gate. Five-ten minutes here or there... but I shall be at the gate. The park is big, so at the main gate only."

"I shall get you, even if you are lost,"—she also whispered. Her eyes glittered. Underneath lay buried the frustration of not qualifying for the medal, depression of adversities at home. The glitter, however, shone more and more... she could feel the warmth. Lest someone should snatch it, she ran out immediately, just as a child runs away after getting his favourite sweet, holding it tight.

"I thought you wanted to say something to me... which you don't get the chance and privacy to do." Prem Prakash told her in the park.

She looked at him with askance—did she really, if so, what was it? She was just looking at him with searching eyes.

"You want to say something?"

"No... nothing in particular."

"That day on phone, you told me all kinds of things about the conduct of your husband."

"Later on, I was surprised at myself, ashamed too."

"Did you tell all that to someone else also?"

"Do you tell such things to any X, Y, Z?"

"I mean someone intimate... friend, female friend."

"I don't have any."

"Inadvertently to someone?"

"No."

"Then why to me...?"

"Don't know. I didn't give it a thought beforehand. Had I... would not have told you. Probably, that day, I was under too much pressure. You felt amiss?"

"No... take out, whenever under pressure, you should take it out. You appear to be an outgoing type – free, roaming about cheerfully, but deep inside, you are sad, depressed all the time."

Instantly, she became tearful. Prem Prakash patted her on the shoulder. "You need a friend. Till you come to have, you can take me as one."

She looked at Prem Prakash with watery eyes... as if trying to explore, measure him. Then her gaze turned towards an old middle-sized hedge before her. The hedge, caged in wires, was of delicate branches. Cut to round shape, it was of the size of a small tree, looked like a man behind bars. Cut regularly from here and there, it has been brought down to proportionate roundness. Its leaves were dusty. Hence, it looked stale. A bird squeaking, hopped to and fro on its frail branches.

"Won't you say something?" Prem Prakash cajoled.

"It is nice sitting here with you," she was stuck with the hedge cast in the image of Prem Prakash.

"But you are not even looking at me."

"What difference does it make. You are there."

There was quietness. Prem Prakash did not pester her further... human being is not a machine that you press the button and it is on. He felt that, at that moment, she has outgrown her age... grown up inwardly. She, on her part, was trying to hold on to the moments which were passing by, for they were precious. She was living them.

"I just can't believe that I am sitting here with you in this park." She murmured, as if to herself.

"Why? What is so special about it? Since we didn't have the privacy to talk at home, we came over here. Everyone does that."

"Yes... but everyone is not lucky to be with you."

"Don't talk about me as others do."

"Not that you are a celebrity or rich... but that you are gifted with compassion. No one cared to stop for me. Everyone thinks that grief in any case will be my fate because I happen to be a woman, a wife at that. That day I was so much shaken that I spoke to you whatever, I don't even remember and you got so much perturbed that you remember everything till this day."

"Was it something which came unexpectedly, vanished soon and shall not come again... a phenomenon temporary?"

"No, it is in place, comes repeatedly. Couldn't tell anybody. Surprising that I told you. How could I gather the courage? The real problem is my being in an environment, totally against my nature – the religious environment, ritualistic. Tell me, when God has not given me anything, why should I have faith in Him and if there is no faith or conviction, why should I partake in the rituals of worship? I have to participate in the rituals of the temple because I am 'Guruain', a priestess. My husband took deeksha, ordained by his 'Guru' and, in turn, he forced it on me. Now I have to sit with him in all the rituals. Even elderly people touch my feet, because I am 'Guruain'... despite my being an atheist. If my atheism is noticed by some, my husband's reputation would get tarnished – what kind of a priest, who couldn't influence even his wife! Daily I participate in an absurd drama. I also deceive those innocent people, who with utter humility come to worship."

An arc of anguish appeared on her face.

"The solution of this problem is very simple – just don't take part in the rituals, if you don't have faith. Tell them clearly that your heart is not in it."

"Can I say that? The position of women in our society – you don't know."

"I know..."

"You don't. You might have read, heard from others. You can write about it, but you can't feel it unless you are a woman... of that particular class, of that society. In my house, the three persons – my husband, both in-laws – are beings apart but have one thing in common – the way they feel it is their inherent right to torture me, wife of one and daughter-in-law of two. All the three agree that first and last I am a daughter-in-law. They torture in different ways. Father-in-law – anyone would say he is a gentleman – would not say anything directly, but would hurl blows of hot wind, as it were. Anytime, in passing, he would murmur – 'the old and retired are made to work in this house; would get a loaf of bread only after hard labour since morning; my mother used to get up at four in the morning, these days daughters-in-law sleep till noon' things like that. The mother-in-law attacks directly. Eyebrows raised, looking angrily, with bitter voice, she would say – 'the blighter rattles like a scissor, knows that I am constrained, left only with one son. Else I would have cut her tongue, then and there. We used to touch the feet of our in-laws every morning. The blighter doesn't bother. For her we are only insignificant insects. She lives in luxury thanks to us. It is my husband's pension that runs the house. The big house where you rule like a queen – who got it constructed – my husband.'

And my husband – he is always busy manoeuvring that his wife remains throughout, within the confinements of the house, made to work like a maid. 'Want to go to the market, what would our parents say, think it over' – is his pet comment? Daily I wash his thick red Swamiji's dress – lungi, kurta, the upper sheet – and press them. A washing machine can reduce my labour. If I propose to buy it, he would say – 'when the upper room was being constructed, we said we had no money; father then had managed all by himself. What would he say now if we buy the washing machine? Think it over'. He would push me forward even in areas meant for gents – 'you go, talk to those people, settle.' Sometimes he would abuse, talk foul, even slap me and only five minutes thereafter, standing on the staircase, would whistle – 'shoo-shoo, throwing up his hands would say 'forget it'. Is it so easy to forget? Anyone can cut a dirty joke at the expense of his wife... he doesn't care, nor bother about her security. He is concerned only with husband's rights. For anything, his pet retort is – 'he committed the mistake of getting me educated'. It is true that B.A. onwards, my education was resumed only after marriage and he paid for it, but to press it every now and then? In between my studies, they wanted a child, mother-in-law growling – "how long we keep rubbing our hands, what did we get of our son's marriage, we need something to play with." Fed up, I bore a child for them, while studying. Those days I didn't sleep for nights together. Result? Everyone is unhappy with me today. Their common complaints are that I don't sit in the temple, don't sweep the house, don't attract people or chat with females to build up Panditji's clientele and clad in red am not in the temple for larger part of the day."

As if muttering all this only to herself, she stopped there. The suppressed ire had come out, her face turning red. Had Prem Prakash not been there, she would have spat... just there.

The sociologist in Prem Prakash was analysing – she from the middle class of a small town in a backward province, where women, including herself till the other day, remained uneducated or almost so. Changing times... that soon after marriage, it pinched her and she aspired to get higher education. She was born with a sharp mind, was industrious... so completed postgraduation with distinction. Yet the concept of a daughter-in-law over there was very traditional – a maid to serve many and keep everyone happy. By mistake, if she happens to think about herself – her being, her life – she is taken to be depraved. India might have moved on, progressed a lot economically, unfortunately this middle-class-town mentality has not changed. She started questioning as a child comes of age suddenly... was looked down upon – this girl, how dare she!

Living in that house, she might go mad.

"You should go out more often, should do a job."

She didn't say a word. Prem Prakash too got alarmed. In our country, is it that easy to get a job? Even if a life hangs on getting a job, it won't come by. But why...

Someone yelled inside him, while she sat speechless, looking at the same tree-like hedge, entangled in the surrounding wires. There was dust on its leaves. The bird jumping and searching something was not there any longer. Little away on the brick pavement, one or two persons having a walk passed by.

"Do you like this city?" She asked after a while. She had changed the topic.

"Shall we call it a city, or just a big town?"

"Whatever... can call it a settlement as well."

"They are all the same. Everywhere there is pollution, mosquitoes, dirty polythene bags flying here and there. What matters is how do you settle yourself there."

"How have you...?"

"I sat down with my work under a tree – you may take it that way."

"In life, is there nothing except work?"

"Why not... you have to decide as to what is important for you at a juncture."

"What is in a life like mine where nothing moves at all, things are going to remain the same."

"It is not like that. See, your life is also moving forward. What was it before your marriage, what is it thereafter. Before your studies and after; before your child and afterwards. Just now, you have one child. When you come to have two or three, you would be different. You have different things to do at different periods of time."

" What is it for me right now?"

"You are just completing your studies. Education has awakened in you the curiosity to know about yourself. You are doing it also – trying to know what you are, what do you want of your life."

"Where everything is going to be determined by circumstances, such efforts signify nothing and, for your information, I am not doing any such thing."

"Efforts such as these are seldom deliberate. Education will make your subconscious do it, wily-nilly."

"Right now, I see only one advantage of education. Am able to see a little outside, meet people like you. Do you think any person in circumstances such as mine can have any expectation from life?"

"A lot. But it is you who will decide. It would happen with the passage of time. Circumstances are never so powerful that no scope is left for possibilities. Shall we leave now..."

"Yes."

"You can come to me whenever you feel like or can send for me anywhere. You share with me whatever... repose faith in me. Don't feel that you are alone. Don't get dejected."

Prem Prakash put his hand on her head. Her hair were thick, black and shining; fairness of the face below looked all the more subdued. Her hands were fairer than her face, feet fairer than hands. Inherent colour of hers was bright, albeit shadowed by dark.

They got up. Her eyes had a little glint then – she was after all walking with Prem Prakash on her side. It gave her fulfillment.

Red attire... she despised. Before she could express her belief fearlessly, she had to throw away the big lie that lay in her conduct. As soon as it dawned on her, she stopped attending evening's 'Aarti', where her presence everyday was a must. Her absence was noted the very first day. The young guru cornered her.

"Didn't come for Aarti, are you alright?"

"Yes."

"Then...?"

"Didn't. Won't come in future too. I don't feel like."

The young guru was shocked. Controlling himself, however, he asked in a composed way. "And why won't you?"

"If you don't have faith, all this is sham, deceiving others."

"Who is deceiving, who doesn't have faith – you or me?"

"I am talking about myself."

"Faith comes from these rituals – by performing puja, partaking in religious ceremonies daily. All this should go on, faith – the type you want – would follow."

"No, I think, faith is first, rituals acquire meaning only thereafter."

"Oh! So you have started thinking too, educated as you are now!"

She was quiet. The young guru continued.

"But what would people think when they don't see you there – you didn't give it a thought – how would they feel?"

"How does it concern me – if those people don't matter to me? Should I care for what they feel or what I do? Anyway, I am not that big a guy that people would miss me there. Slowly they would get used to it."

"And the 'puja', which goes incomplete that way?"

"You are there performing in all its details. It would be complete."

"We have been performing evening 'Aarti' as a couple."

"If I don't have faith of that level, my participation itself pollutes it."

"Are you ashamed of sitting with your husband in religious ceremonies?"

"Me, qua wife...what is there to be ashamed, but me, qua Guruain, a priestess.... I am certainly ashamed of it because I am not worthy of it."

"So, you will not sit with me in any ceremony?"

"I will... in the domestic, as all wives do but not in the temple where I have to sit as a Guruain, a priestess."

"We both have taken 'deeksha' (apprenticeship) from the same guruji. If we do not worship together, you will be cursed."

"I will be cursed, not you. You continue observing the conditions of 'deeksha'. I cannot..."

"Why can't you? How have you been doing so far? What has happened all of a sudden?"

"Nothing suddenly. For years, the conflict has been going on. I thought I shall develop faith. I couldn't, I have taken this decision after lot of deliberations."

But why now... why didn't it happen earlier?"

"Everything has its own timing. The time came and it happened."

"What would Guruji think, when he comes to know?"

"He would appreciate that I couldn't manage the rigours of his 'Deeksha'. Otherwise, too, he has better things to do than think about me."

"You will be guilty of blasphemy."

"Not you... me only."

"So, you have started thinking separately,"

"I am your wife but a separate being too. Do you always think what I do? Then, why that expectation from me?"

"Feathers have started growing on you – I see that."

The young guru said it with angry crookedness and to divert himself, he moved over to sit before the T.V.

That day, she came to Prem Prakash's home unannounced. She went to his mother and wife first but didn't stay there for long. Formalities over, she came to Prem Prakash's study. Entering she wished him a little loudly. Forgetting to respond, Prem Prakash got lost in her glittering eyes. She sat down on the chair opposite.

"Was going to fetch my son from the school. Had some time, thought of passing by this way."

"Good. So, how are you?"

"How do I look?"

"Appear to be good."

She was dressed in salwar and half-sleeves red kurta with white artistry on its neck and sleeves. The kurta was short and tight – probably made much earlier, when she might have been in 12th standard or so. She looked attractive in it. Below the dupatta, attention was perforce drawn towards the upper portion of her arms – fair and fleshy. From the tight kurta, fairness drooped down to merge in the smoothness of the lower portion of the arms. Light red dupatta and white decorative artistry on the sleeves of her kurta combined to cast an attractive glow on her beautiful arms.

"Writing something new...?"

"Something or the other goes on... a thing left over – may take shape, may not. But whatever... it does cast its shadow on our thinking, on our personality, and, of course, on what is being written currently. What do you say...."

"What can I? Could have said something, had I been a professional writer."

"Even if not so, you are a human being alright, living and kicking. It happens with each one of us, maybe a little more deeply with us, professionals. That's all."

She was deliberating – Prem Prakash talks more of the future. What is her future? What beckons her... is there something? Weighed down by the past, threatened by the present, she has hardly any future. She, however, continued. "Yes... and that's what makes the difference. There are so many who do not think at all – are not able to, educated ones too, eat, drink and be merry type. I envy such people. The likes of me are compelled by life to think... but are unable to think clearly and consistently. We give up midway, because our thinking does not appear to make any dent in our lives. You people persist... and, thus, are able to arrive.... achieve clarity in your thoughts."

"On the contrary, I feel I am quite confused."

"May be inside, outside you are quite clear."

"How do you know?"

"From what you say? Even if you do not speak, your presence, your personality speaks. Vibrations!"

"My wife feels otherwise. She curses herself ten times a day for being an intellectual's wife," Prem Prakash laughed.

"A person sleeping under the tree does not feel its flavour, while a passerby invariably does."

"Enough... enough! Tell me, is everything alright on that front?"

"Which front?"

"Your house..."

"Yes, O.K... as far as it can be."

She got up, was not interested to talk about it. She walked over to an almirah, started scanning the books there but soon moved on to another where honours conferred on Prem Prakash were displayed. This was the outermost portion of the study and the house from where you could get out to the verandah, lawns beyond and parallel to the exit gate. This part of the study was not visible from inside the house. Quite often, she bent over to have a closer look at things, sometimes to read what was inscribed on various medals and mementoes.

Her slim figure accentuated in her tight clothes – curve of the trim waist, round hips rising behind, legs getting still thinner as they drooped down... that fair ankle too sometimes peeped out.

Prem Prakash couldn't resist – his gaze stuck at her bare arms – smooth and fair, there fleshy roundness acquiring a golden hue as they drooped down from the red kurta. From his position, the arms looked all the more fair and full.

"Wow! You got so many awards and honours..." bursting with joy she said, her eyes still caught in the almirah.

Prem Prakash was pulled towards her. Throwing a quick look through the inside door that no one was around, he clasped her from behind. Holding her beautiful arms, he clung to her hips, his head on her neck. The mellow smell flowing from the roots of her hair filled his nostrils.

His eyes and lips licking her smooth arms by turns – upwards and downwards, he turned her over to his side and kissed her on the lips.

"Aye... Aye... What are you doing..." She separated herself by giving Prem Prakash a strong push, wiped out the kiss by scratching her lips on her kurta and ran out. She was scared, a little angry too, was breathing heavily.

After a while, Prem Prakash too came out, ashamed and in slow gait. By then she has composed herself although her face was still red. A full glance at Prem Prakash and she moved towards a bed of plants in the lawn. She picked up the pipe used for watering the plants, opened the tap and started watering a plant nearby, first on the ground, then on the leaves.

Sensing Prem Prakash nearby, she said – "See, how much dust is there on this poor thing. It is not enough to water on the ground."

She moved over to another plant.

"Plants also want to bathe. If you bathe them like this, how lively they become! See how they are smiling now... matters little that they can't speak."

Prem Prakash saw her lost in plants. He was just behind her, but she felt safe now, having come out in the open. Overlooking the scare and anger that plagued her a few minutes earlier, she turned and said slowly – "Don't get angry; Keep me along."

At that point of time, she could have abused him like anything and Prem Prakash, ashamed as he was, would have taken it all. Despite all his intelligence, Prem Prakash was neither able to understand his own behaviour, nor that of this girl, who right then was watering the plants, her face towards them.

"Oh! 'school-time! I push off..." she cried, handed over the pipe to Prem Prakash and ran away. Prem Prakash heard the sound of the gate opening and closing. A moment later, only the sound of water falling from the pipe in his hands was there.

What a difference between your outer and the real self! The former civilised, well behaved, moral, kind and what not and the real one? A hungry wolf greedy for flesh. You were not drunk but your behaviour certainly was inebriate. It is not for nothing that wine and women are clubbed together. Drinks and the sight of female flesh lead to similar stimulation in men.

Your horoscope was analysed by experts. Everyone, depending on their expertise, underlined the prominence of 'shukra'. The liberals among them opined that thanks to 'shukra', love would be there in your life throughout. A cynic, however, said what after – all can a poor woman—constrained from different directions, bound by different poles – give. As in speech, so in life, that fellow was bit of a crack. He never married, avoided women as one avoids the muck. The third category expert, a little too cruel, was, however, truthful. His opinion was that the 'shukra' in your horoscope is demoniac. All other planets are out to push you up the ladder, but this one pulls you down. It will lead you to a wrong path, will be instrumental in defaming you. Had it not been there, you would have scaled the Everest. In life, you will never be able to get rid of women, or won't like to – it's the same thing.

Funny – you say – if that is your destiny, how are you responsible! If destiny has shaped your nature, it has... what can you do about it. As regards fame, you have already achieved enough. Why should you hanker after more, particularly if you have to go against your nature. Why all the time after fame, progress, as if that be the 'be all and end all'. Why not let yourself flow in accordance with whatever your nature is and in whatever direction it takes? You say if you do not force yourself, why restrain either?

You may secure yourself in the fortress made of your reasoning and logic, but what about fall from grace – where you fall in your own and others' esteem. You proceeded to give her solace and kindness. It was only appearance... as with your social work. To show off is a matter of habit with you. The fact is that you did not feel kindness or any such thing for her. Your focus all the time was on flesh as the prey is for the tiger hiding in the bush or the crocodile lying lifeless on the sands... only to pounce upon at the first opportunity. You also attacked suddenly... 'don't give her any chance'. She, a poor girl, inferior to you in all respects... what could she do except running away.

She was bemoaning the cruelty of her husband to you, thought you were different. She needed you but received only what she gets from her husband. She must be shocked to find you no different, you too after flesh. Does it not make any difference to you that you fell in her estimate so soon?

But why did she say – "don't get angry, keep me along?" What does it mean? To say this when she could have abused you, left and right?

Prem Prakash was indisposed. Guilt tormented him. He could neither openly beg her pardon, nor excuse himself. To top it all she left a riddle with him, "keep me along." Despite all his knowledge of Social Science, he could not solve that riddle, which kept coming to him repeatedly. She did not say – "Keep me with you, or, keep me in your company." Instead – "Keep me along," implying moving forward, under his care. Is she so choosy about words, or they just got picked up by her innocence as out of dirt, particles of grain are pecked out by a bird in natural course. Did they have some intent? It would not have mattered much, had she consciously used them. Then the design behind would have come out. Those words came to her subconsciously and, hence, they must have some meaning which even she did not know.

She came running as soon as she learnt about Prem Prakash's illness. He was lying on the cot in his study. Reaching straight to him, she sat down on the cot beside him and put her palm on his forehead – 'what happened, why fever?... headache, should I press?' Had she not been present herself that sentimentality would have looked out of sorts. She was really distressed. Love, kindness were reflected in her eyes. While putting it away, Prem Prakash's lips naturally came to her palm from inside. It was damp over there... as if her sensitivity and affability had descended on it. Just then, Prem Prakash's mother and wife came from inside. Neither she nor Prem Prakash was on the line of their gaze, which was directed straight to the place where she sat – in the middle of the cot from where her clothes, if not her body, almost touched Prem Prakash. In their perception, it was shamelessness on the part of a girl; it was apparent from their piercing eyes' glance... but she didn't bother even to look at them. Sitting there, she continued asking Prem Prakash about illness, medicines, etc. She got up only when she had to go out for fetching water to enable Prem Prakash to take the medicine. On return, she sat down on the chair opposite and got occupied in the formal talks about illness, doctors, medicines, etc. When they were alone again, Prem Prakash muttered in a slow tone –

"Pardon me for my behaviour that day. It was surely despicable."

"So, that's it. You have fallen ill thinking about all those things. Don't you have better things to think about?"

"What have you thought about employment?"

"As you say. But I want to do Ph.D. right now."

"You may do it along with your job. I have in view a private institute of journalism. One Vermaji is all in all there. See him any day after tomorrow, after seeking appointment. I will give you his phone number and also brief him about you."

"First you recover..."

"I have only to get up and phone. Will you have to consult at home?"

"There is no one who is worthy of it but since I would be going out of the house to serve for the first time, I think..."

"Yes, you should... but you are inclined alright?"

"For what...?"

"For taking up a job, what else!"

"You felt I should do it, the matter ends there for me."

"It isn't proper to trust someone so early. So far you even don't know me... I am wicked as you have witnessed."

She didn't respond. Distraught she was looking here and there.

"One should not trust someone so much – Prem Prakash reiterated." Learn to decide for yourself, with own wisdom."

"If my wisdom directs me to follow you...?"

"This is not wisdom but blind faith. You should yourself deliberate and decide, you alone understand your life, yourself too."

"I understand neither. Thinking is not my forte. Could not develop it because I was discouraged from the very beginning... and am even now. You are the first to suggest that I should think. Right now, I want to complete my Ph.D."

"That you can do along with your job. I favour service because it would enable you to get out of the suffocating atmosphere at your house; you would be away the whole day. But you must ask them. I think only thereafter should I send you to Vermaji. If you so wish, I can talk to your husband."

"As you choose."

"Again! again you leaned upon whatever was said?"

"It will take little time to change..."

"I think it would be better if I talk to him. That way I shall be a witness to whatever controversy relating to your taking up a job may arise in future. I shall be able to assert that they were consulted alright."

They switched over to the topic of illness because Prem Prakash's mother and wife reappeared at that point. Although her service was not a topic which could not be discussed before them, yet how could they talk about it before those who could not even bear the sight of her sitting on the cot of Prem Prakash.

Prem Prakash phoned her husband to know his views about her doing a job. The young guru was exhilarated, extremely grateful – she doesn't come to the temple... so, besides doing the domestic chores, if she also brings in some money... the better. Mouth full of sweetness – as was his wont, his face round as a rasgulla – he said –

"It will be really nice. Need your blessings!"

"Would she have time?"

"Why not... What is she doing whole day long except sitting idle at home? Need your blessings!"

Prem Prakash felt peeved; he knew that she overstretches herself doing the domestic chores.

The young guru, easily passed on his responsibility to Prem Prakash by repeating – 'need your blessings'. Prem Prakash envied this man who with the help of just a few words lived carefree. On any matter he would say to his wife, 'You see it, think it over' and the responsibility is passed over to her; would say "exactly...exactly" a hundred times to the devotees, implying that he was only confirming their views. If he has to seek something from someone, he would repeat – 'need your blessings'. Whenever he picked the phone and Prem Prakash happened to ask what was she doing, he with profound satisfaction would observe – 'she is cooking' or 'she is washing clothes'. Wife doing chores inside, husband leisurely sitting outside, watching T.V., talking on phone or feet resting on table just glancing through the newspaper – any life better than that?

She was doing a job now, getting out of the house everyday, but it didn't bring about any basic change in her. Self-confidence... she had it earlier. She didn't feel much obliged to Prem Prakash. She thought she anyway was too qualified for the job he got for her. She worked harder than expected, worth more than the salary she received, devoted more time and energy than any of her colleagues did. Her visits to Prem Prakash were more frequent now, not because he had got her the job or she hoped he would be useful to her in future also, but because she genuinely liked being with him, could talk all sorts of things with him, and without reservations. She found herself in agreement with much of what he said, felt that she could trust him. Prem Prakash once advised her not to use lip-stick, for it takes away the natural colour of lips. She stopped it. Later on, however, she found herself debating within – why natural colour, for whom? Surely not for husband she despised. Was Prem Prakash asking it for himself? Having been pushed away that day by her, he has not done anything untoward since. Once when he was alone in the house, he asked her to stay on. She politely declined – "Sir, my home, whatever, is something to me. I live there. From wherever, I have to return to it daily. God knows for how long more have I to stay there, with them... so I have to follow the rules. I always reach there before it gets dark."

"But you don't agree with those rules, don't like your in-laws."

"I hate each one of them. Outwardly, however, I have to play the role of a wife, a daughter-in-law."

"I don't know whether you have that in you – playing roles."

"I know it's not in me... and my rebellion comes out in my personal behaviour with them. I don't hide it either. Whatever be the state of my relationship with them, both have to face it. But, outwardly, I maintain the decorum for their honour's sake and this is a favour I do them. That way I am repaying their loan for allowing me to complete my education. Respectable conduct outwardly may also be helplessness because there is no alternative for me.

"In relation to me also, do you feel forced?"

"No, I come to you because I want to. Truly speaking, you have put life in me, who otherwise was dead. You have taught me to think... about myself, my life."

"Learnt it?"

"Have started. The process of thinking has set in atleast. It may or may not lead anywhere but has commenced alright. Earlier, nothing used to happen."

"And what's that you often say – "Keep me with you or keep me along." What do you mean?"

"I need to be with you. So, I come running whenever you call. I come on my own too. Have understood this much that if I am lucky to remain with you, I would live."

"But on your own, you never propose to meet or meet somewhere outside."

"I don't withhold myself either. I come whenever and wherever you ask me to. However, I don't want to burden you. If I say – 'Keep me with you', it is with full awareness of the fact that I cannot give you anything, am not worthy of you from any point of view, am of no use to you."

"How do you know that you are of no use? I feel attracted towards you. You must have sensed."

"Yes and I wanted to tell you – there is nothing in me. You appear to have desire for the physical. I don't have it. It died... that is not correct, for it never existed. From the very beginning, my circumstances were such that it was never born; it was nipped in the bud. What I saw of him from the very beginning, hatred for men got deeply ingrained in me. Don't know how I came close to you... here too I have distaste for the physical. I think, in course of time, you too will lose interest in me on that count. I don't want to hurt you, but can't help it."

Is it possible to move forward from here... if so, where to? If I do – and I know she won't object – it would be like charging fee for getting her employed. So, I must withdraw. She is already so aggrieved, can't be hurt further. My company for her only up to the point where she gets strength to live.

One day, she told Prem Prakash that her husband and in-laws are selling their present house and buying another. It is a bit far, but is cheaper and more spacious. As it is a property matter, it would be better if Prem Prakash oversees it. Prem Prakash immediately shrugged off –

"See... only that which is related to you and your life, matters to me. What your family members do is no concern of mine. It is their money, their property, they may do whatever they like. Yes, if you proceed to invest your money and you consult me, I may...."

"My money... Where is it..."

"The pay you get, four thousand a month. You get cheque or cash?

"Cash."

"What do you do with it?"

"Give to my husband. What else? He passes it on to his mother – sometimes full, sometimes a little less."

Prem Prakash was annoyed. Was it this that he got her employed for – that she may add to the family income? Had she deposited it in a bank account, she would have created a balance that would have increased her self-confidence. He could not imagine her to be so foolish. Women deposit their earnings separately. It is the husband who has to run the house... if the wife were not earning, he had to run it in any case. Thus, it is that a woman's earnings are hers as is the money received in marriage – 'stree-dhan'. Legally also it is so. But see this lady – on the one hand, she despises her husband, his family, rebels too but puts her full monthly pay obediently at their disposal.

"What about your personal expenses?"

"Whenever I need something, I ask money for it – say, for scooty, petrol, my dress or son's..."

"Means, despite earning, you keep begging."

She didn't say anything, taking Prem Prakash's irritation quietly. It softened Prem Prakash – what can the poor thing do if her family has that kind of middle-class arrangement in their house. Earlier, joint families had it – just like kitchen, money had also to be common but then women were not earning. She has gone out to earn and at home she is putting up with the system of joint families. It has been cleverly invoked by her family – make her earn with no right on her earnings.

"Have you opened your account in the bank?"

"No, what shall I put there?"

"If not your entire salary, at least part... after keeping the required cash with yourself for your personal expenditure."

"They know my salary. Whether I put whole or part, there will be ill-will. It will be the moment I open bank account in my name at all. They would say – 'what is this – mine and thine? Does your husband have any brother that it is called for? Everything belongs to him and so is yours...' But I know – nothing is mine. My education was upto intermediate when I got married. I completed my graduation and postgraduation after marriage and, for that, my husband repeatedly makes me feel obliged that it was he who got me educated. I always thought that someday I shall repay this debt. If I give them my salary, I feel I am repaying that debt and I am also paying for my boarding and lodging in their house."

"Will anyone give you credit for it?"

"Let them not. I have the satisfaction alright. If they overtorture, I can always say that I am not their dependent, I deposit with them every month in advance, more than what they spend on me."

What self-respect! Prem Prakash was astonished, advised her politely.

"See, the situation you are in, it is necessary that you have your bank account. Bank balance would give you confidence."

"Confidence – does it come with bank balance?"

"What else...?"

"I get it from you..."

She was looking deep into Prem Prakash's eyes. Her face had reddened, she could feel the heat on her face.

"Yes...that's true," she said after a pause, "I feel very confident when you are around."

Prem Prakash felt irritated. Dependence on the house is fast turning dependence on him... and he is instrumental for that.

"See, you have to be self-dependent. Having one's own bank balance – whatever the amount – is the first step. Now, will you open your own bank account?"

"Yes... if you say. When I do coaching or tuition, I shall put that money too in my account."

"Precisely! I know your situation, will get your account opened quietly. They will come to know only later on."

"Will you kindly look at that property matter."

"I told you. That matter pertains to them, not to you. Let us draw a line here – whatever relates to you, or affects you, I shall intervene... not in all matters of your family."

She didn't press it further. Was not disappointed or angry either. She thought – ultimately it is Prem Prakash who has to take a call on it. He can't be compelled. No one asked him to get her employed. He himself felt like doing it.

Barely a month after... Prem Prakash noticed turmoil in her house. She had not told him anything. While on morning walk, he casually dropped in her house and her father-in-law narrated the story. The young guru, relying too much on one of his pupils, had signed and got his father also to sign the sale agreement of their present house. As per the agreement, the buyer had to part with only a small amount in the beginning, the rest was to be paid after the house was handed over. Registration was to be made in the name of whosever, decided by the purchaser. Obviously, the agreement was done by some middleman, who would sell out the house to some other person, would raise some money for himself in between. Her family had booked a new house but payment for the same had to come from the sales proceeds of the present house. The possession of new house was to be available only on full payment. Following the sales agreement, these people were being coerced to vacate the house, where they were living even before the full payment had been made. Were they to do so, it was also not certain that they would get the major part of the agreed sales proceeds.

Now the ruffians sent by the middlemen would come every alternate day, cite the sales agreement, threaten, abuse and ask them to vacate, else they would throw them out. At times, the poor girl had to come out and face the hooligans... she a woman... and she never once mentioned it.

When alone with her, Prem Prakash complained – "Why didn't you tell me?"

"You desired to be kept away from this matter."

"I had also said – whatever affects you..."

"And look at this man. He trusted his pupil so much that whatever he brought, this fellow blindly signed it. Can't judge a man. His father is also at fault – he was more experienced, couldn't he stop it? It is his property, why did he sign? And now, I have to suffer the consequences. Whosoever comes threatening, I have to face, else these people might agree to vacate. Where would I go with my child and household, move on to the street? Man provides security to his wife and, look at him – he has just done the opposite. Says let us vacate, would live somewhere for a few days; as soon as our house is ready, shall shift there."

She was on fire. Her face was red, eyes swollen. Probably, she had not slept for days, wept when alone.

"Now he says he committed a mistake and I should now correct it. He created the mess, I should clear it."

"O.k...o.k., now relax" Prem Prakash tried to pacify.

"How can I" – she now took on Prem Prakash – "how can one live with this man, who is bent upon throwing his wife and son on the street."

Prem Prakash, for the first time, saw her so agitated – her tender frame stretching to the limit in anger and agitation, shrill voice getting hoarse each time she raised its pitch, her body uncared, going helter-skelter, eyes swollen, red spots below them. Her frail frame shook when she spoke... as a tiny branch under the storm, shaking and straining to the breaking point... just to hold on somehow.

Prem Prakash called for the agreement and studied it carefully. Then he counselled young guru.

"See brother, this agreement clearly favours them. To give possession of the house only on receipt of an insignificant part of the sales proceeds – is simply not done. Take it for certain that if you give possession of the house to them without getting full amount, you will not get a penny later on."

"He says take post-dated cheques."

"Then keep running after them. You are purchasing a new house. Would your vendor agree to take post-dated cheques from you?"

"I asked him. He says they do not have any such system."

"Then. It is also laid down in this agreement that on scrapping it, you shall pay interest at the rate of 18 per cent on whatever money you received from them."

"I know – mistake has been committed by us."

"So now, first you must resolve that, come what may, you shall not vacate this house till the entire amount has been paid."

"But the agreement says that the full amount will be paid only on giving vacant possession and registration."

"May be. You tell them – where do we go? If they pay the full amount, you will get your new house and shift there. This house should be handed over to them only on full payment. You have to remain firm on this, whatever the agreement."

"He says some day he will come with a gang and throw us out."

"How come! This is only an agreement to sell. The house as yet has not been sold. It is yours... until full payment, registration, etc. How can anyone throw you out from your own house? You have to hold on with courage. You have not to vacate till you get the full payment."

You came away... advising them to hold on boldly, but when ruffians would descend on their house, who shall face them?... She, who else? Did you do something for her? This time you didn't tell her straight that the matter pertains to her in-laws, hence they have to tackle... because you had to feign that you are helping. You need such pretensions because you are in social service. But you must have noticed now – social service in association with some institution is one thing, it is quite another to actually handle a real-life situation, help a living being. You wanted to show others, yourself too, that you are full of what they call milk of kindness. You have read that essay – 'The Cuckoo's nest' – the cuckoo deluding itself about raising the chicks, whereas the crows are actually doing it! Yours is the kind of social service which officers' wives do – instead of developing within the genuine feeling of serving, keep convincing yourself that you are indeed engaged in something big – selfless social service! Are you any better than the cuckoo or the officers' wives?

A smart guy indeed you are. First you secure yourself by drawing a circle around you. You help, operating from within that circle only, fully ensuring that no harm comes to you in the least, while you continue to get the 'kick' of helping others. Here you will fight their battle, sitting safe in your circle... but 'kuru-shetra' is there my dear... their house. Why don't you go there?

You always convince yourself that you immediately reach where you see pain. In fact, it is only a show-off... for those around, this time for her.

If you have got yourself involved in this fuss for her sake because you feel for her, nothing wrong; no problem about helping her, but why half-heartedly? You counselled and came away. Why did you withdraw when she had initially requested you to see the papers relating to the sale of the property? Had you seen then, this situation would not have arisen. You thought that you will involve yourself only where she is affected. Now you see – who is affected most in this entire episode, who is the most insecure?

Why should it not be assumed that, in this matter, you are as much a culprit as her husband, her father-in-law.

I should have associated myself when she had initially requested. Then I would have definitely insisted upon seeing the agreement before they put their signatures on it and laid my fingers on the trap laid out. Anyone would have. The young guru signed on trust of his pupil and father on son's. Even she could have noticed the catch, had she seen the draft. That much education and intelligence she has. Probably, she also lost interest once I declined. I didn't agree to her request, even though she hinted that some trap might be there. She had the premonition that something untoward would happen. She knew her husband.

Why remorse now? Once she has candidly told that physical pleasures do not very much interest her, being friend to her remains the only possibility – where she can seek my advice on any matter, accept if deemed fit. She feels secure with me as her guide. Nothing wrong about being interested in those around us, contributing something to their lives. It is much better than selfishly remaining immersed in one's own life. But this relationship is going beyond it.

Why is it so, that she suffers a pain and I feel its pangs. What bond, what relationship is this... any of previous birth which you can't recognise, yet are compelled? She just appeared and her pains became mine. She can hardly give me anything. She may appear to be beautiful sometime from some vantage, but she is so miserable inside that if someone were

to discover beauty in her, will find only pain, nothing else. It appears that from the very beginning, misery has torn her apart. She is the picture of a person who falls, gets up somehow only to fall again. Caught in this web, what can she give?

Why is it so that any misery befalling her and a wound opens up in me and then as if someone with a thread pulls a thin needle across the wound...slowly and so painfully!

Prem Prakash, who once sat aloof, was now running as if the calamity had befallen him. He tried to influence the opposite party through an officer – that they stop all this, pay the full amount and take over the house as normally done. Sales agreement is not legally enforceable as signatures of the vendors have been obtained under duress. The party gave an evasive reply to the officer and further increased the pressure on these people. At stake after all was money, earnings for the middlemen, who were not getting a genuine purchaser immediately, else would have taken the higher amount and got the house registered directly in his name. They would then have seized the profit-money and disappeared. Presently, their representatives continued to threaten these people on phone or directly on the spot as before. A message was also sent by them that the officer through whom you have sought to pressurise has already been bribed and neutralised. Hooliganism, abusing didn't stop. Her family was constantly under fear that they would any day throw out the luggage, force them out, take possession of the house and make the whole thing appear as per the agreement. To prevent this, Prem Prakash asked these people to apply to police for security. He also advised the young guru to arrange some of his pupils to sleep in their house at night for a few days, so that their morale is up.

Things went on like this for a few days. The officer, who had sought to influence the opposite party, in the meantime, advised to move the court also. That would act as additional pressure, while he will continue his. It was also proposed to the middlemen that whatever money had been paid by them can be paid back with interest and the sales agreement be cancelled. The party refused; they would only take the house, vacant possession as provided in the sales agreement.

Ultimately, her family engaged a lawyer. Harbhajan was known to them. The young guru regarded him as his guru-bhai as Harbhajan and he, both had taken 'deeksha' from the same Guruji. The young guru continued with the Guruji, while Harbhajan, at an opportune time deserted him. Guruji disowned Harbhajan, while the young guru was his favourite, more so as he invited him for some ceremonies in the temple. Harbhajan, on the other hand, was now nowhere. He could not get a job, so took up practice of law. When young guru approached him, he was sadistically happy. Harbhajan had always felt that it was young guru, who had poisoned the ears of Guruji. The fellow has now come to him for help, that too with his wife. She was not inclined to go but the young guru insisted – "You come... everything now will be as per your advice only, else if anything going a little wrong, you would create havoc!"

"You call it 'little'! Blindly signing the sales agreement!" She had growled, but got ready to accompany him to the lawyer. She had no faith in her husband.

Harbhajan enjoyed teasing them. He would ask them to come in the evening – at an hour when they have to come straight from their offices. Then he would make them sit in his chamber until late at night. Pretending being very busy, he himself would turn up late so that initially too they have to wait. Then his long conversations on the mobile regarding matters unconnected to them, what he called chat with clients, discussions with fellow lawyers. In between, he would prepare his 'gutka' (raw tobacco leaves mixed with lime) several times. For spitting it out, he had kept a 'peekdan' (a utensil specially made for spitting) under his table. To impress these people, he would talk to the opposite party before them. Thus, he impressed the other party too that he was acting in their interest and can mediate. When any such person, who had earlier threatened these people, was online, Harbhajan would invariably make young guru listen to what all he was saying now. This was a clever device of further terrifying these people. Harbhajan had already told them that the other party consisted of people who are real dare-devils, quite a few of them having cases of murder against them and a compromise, if it could be achieved, would be worth it. He, however, was in touch with both sides so that, in the event of a compromise, he could manage brokerage from both. A lawyer's fee is only a tuppence. Thus, it is that eventually legal practice in small places had turned into brokerage. The young guru and his wife had to go to Harbhajan every third day. Sometimes when they came back, it was already past twelve in the night. She used to keep Prem Prakash informed about all. Prem Prakash was scared that the opposite party might attack them on their way back. She, not the young guru, would be the target, for it was she who had faced their abuses and threats and shot back at them. Had she not come in the picture, their plan would have proceeded smoothly.

She sat at the back of the scooter, driven by the young guru. A big hit on her head from behind by another racing scooter... hit and vanish in the dark. No trace!

Prem Prakash had nightmares. He kept himself informed through young guru's phone. Sometimes, he rang up her house at midnight just to ensure that they have reached.

Such anxiety... for whom? She, who else? Prem Prakash was surprised at himself – he who thought of keeping himself out of all this, was now deep into it, having same tensions. How providence had dragged him in?

One day she called to inform Prem Prakash that a communication has to be sent to the opposite party. Harbhajan has called them to sign. If Prem Prakash could take the trouble of accompanying them to Harbhajan, he could have a look before it is signed!

"Would it be below your dignity?" she politely asked after her request.

"What dignity... how come it gets in there?"

"Going to a lawyer."

"Lawyer only... not any thief or a lawbreaker, but I am not any law expert to advise about a legal notice."

"I shall feel confident, if you come along. But be sure you will not feel any inconvenience?"

"No... none at all. But your putting trust in me for everything is what I don't understand."

"I don't know... I just feel that everything will be all right, if you are there."

"This... even though I had not taken any interest in the matter despite your asking for it initially?"

"What happened, has happened. But you agree now that all this would not have happened, had you seen it then."

"May be. It could have been certainly managed at that stage. Now, God knows! O.K., I shall come."

Prem Prakash couldn't refuse. Ascertained time and location of Harbhajan's chamber. They – husband and wife – reached first, Prem Prakash joined later. He noticed that Harbhajan was both an egoist and cunning. While talking to the other party, he put the receiver on young guru's ear. Young guru's face turned pale with fear. A threat was being conveyed from the other end – possession of the house must be given by tomorrow, otherwise they will throw them out."

"How come? The house is not yet sold, only an agreement to sell has been executed" – Prem Prakash objected when the talk on phone was over.

"Sahab! That's how it is. They are wolves... three cases of murder are already against them. They just commit the crime and walk away... law to be taken care of later."

Harbhajan was further scaring them. Prem Prakash felt that outwardly Harbhajan was trying to win their trust by enabling them to overhear the opposite party on his phone; but he might be doing something similar for the opposite party. He might have informed them about this meeting and asked to phone precisely at this time to convey the threats. He made the young guru overhear the threats purposefully. There was a design behind it. He was after compromise rather than litigation. He finally said, "If you say, I withhold this communication and make another attempt for a compromise. How much more should they pay that you give possession of the house?"

"Nothing short of full payment..." Prem Prakash interjected – problem of these people is – where do they go."

"Let them pay the full amount" – sharply she came in – "so that we pay our builder fully and get the house we are purchasing. They should give us three days' time thereafter to move to the new house."

"But bhabhi! All this is not provided in your agreement."

"Let not! Tell me sincerely – do you really think whatever is written here should be carried out, possession of the house to be given even before the full payment is made. This is not done even when you go to buy vegetables. Here it is a house."

"But there is an agreement which bears your signature, of the Attorney."

"Can't we get the agreement cancelled? Prem Prakash suggested.

"They, not we, can do it. They shall have a ground to cancel... when you violate any of its stipulations, e.g., not giving possession of the house by the due date, even though they made the payment of the amount agreed to. What ground do we have to cancel?"

"That which is the truth – that signatures have been obtained deceptively" – she was participating in the discussion as equal now. Prem Prakash got a point.

"She is right. Make this the main ground. Put other things too. We give them the notice to cancel this agreement."

"What do you want – to sell the house or keep it?" Harbhajan asked.

The young guru's circular face has grown all the more round for having kept quiet so long. She was looking at Prem Prakash, who was hesitant. It was their family matter after all.

"Let us be clear on one thing. It will not be easy to sell the house later on. It will be reported as disputed. Besides, how many in this town are capable of paying such big amount. So, we should find some way that the house is sold as desired and we also do not suffer," Harbhajan was reasoning.

"If this house is not sold, we will not be able to pay the instalments for our new house; there will be interest for non-payment. If we do not take the new house, whatever money we have so far paid for it – around 2 lakhs will be forfeited. Think all that." The young guru was counseling his wife. Prem Prakash was surprised that the fellow thinks about everything, except the suffering which will be caused to his family.

"How have you entrapped yourself from all sides!"

Prem Prakash couldn't help observing. The young guru blushed.

"Now tell me quickly please." – Harbhajan was insistent – "They will send their men day after. If you wish, I can get you some more time, now on phone."

Harbhajan appeared to be a strange lawyer. He was engaged by these people but was playing games for the opposite party. Prem Prakash had to tell him candidly – "See, the house is still the property of these people as the sale has not yet taken place, registration not done. Why should they vacate? Are they tenants? Even if they think of vacating, where do they go to live. The crux lies here. They can vacate only when they get possession of the new house. That they will get when full payment thereof is made. Let the opposite party pay the full amount, which these people pay off to their builder. They get the house, move there. The matter ends."

"The opposite party will not make the full payment?"

"Why?"

"Because they don't have the money."

"Then get this agreement cancelled. We shall see whatever follows."

"What Bhabhi, what do you say? "Harbhajan asked her. "Cancel..." In one word, she conveyed her decision.

Harbhajan now had nothing to say. Had he persisted even now, it would become obvious that he was acting for the other party – which he didn't want to show. He, therefore, made a U-turn immediately.

"I had actually got ready a notice to this effect only... see...

Prem Prakash took the draft, which had numerous corrections here and there. The content on the whole was o.k. Only circumstances in which the signatures had been obtained had to be further underlined. Prem Prakash advised Harbhajan suitably.

"Now Bhabhi! You sit here beside me and type fair, as I go on dictating."

That is – one hour more. Prem Prakash had helped them decide about cancellation. But if the opposite party carries out its threat, sends ruffians to throw them out day after... something has to be done for that.

"This notice will go only tomorrow. You bring it with you to your house. We shall see it there and sign. Right now I have to go somewhere. I come to your house tomorrow morning at seven," Prem Prakash told her.

He didn't leave any further scope for the lawyer. He knew that once he had decided, she would strictly go by it only. She was stubborn that way. Harbhajan could also not counter.

Leaving Harbhajan's chamber, Prem Prakash had the satisfaction that whatever decision has been taken, it was not exclusively his. It was of Prem Prakash and hers. He made an opening and she followed as she always did. No distraction was called for now. On the whole, it was a right decision, because the focus was on the human plight, monetary aspect kept aside. These people will now not be on the road. Despite this satisfaction, Prem Prakash was tense. While driving back, he was sweating all over.

Decision has been taken alright but the responsibility now has shifted this side – over to me. Harbhajan would definitely convey to the opposite party that notice of cancellation is on the way. If before getting the notice, they get bent upon throwing them out forcibly? What security is there for these people... and now she, her husband, inlaws will only look to me for everything I have taken over the responsibility and now a cliff hangs above. Even if I stay in their house tomorrow, all the day long, can I face the goons alone? It is one thing to win

over the lawyer to your side, quite another to fight the goons. Now it is my problem. I pulled it over to my side.

Strangely enough, there is no repentance. Seems it had to happen, should have happened much earlier. Her problem is my problem. She in misery and I remaining aloof... this is just unnatural, as water not flowing on the slope, or earth not absorbing water!

Prem Prakash repeatedly took out the hankie to wipe out the perspiration on his forehead but was drenched inside. Years before he might have passed through such tension, but had later on learnt to remain composed; he was no longer habituated to such ups and downs.

Suddenly, he remembered a friend who happened to be a police officer and his car took the turn to his residence. He can be requested to provide security to these people for a couple of days.

Notice for cancellation of the sales agreement followed by the cheque for repayment of the money advanced by them along with interest, softened the opposite party. They had banked on the premise that these people being a weak party, can be coerced to hand over the house, which could then be sold out on profit to a third party. That profit and additionally the amount ultimately not paid to these people was to be theirs. They were silenced when these people turned out to be adamant with support behind. The sales agreement got automatically cancelled once the last date given for reply expired. Thereafter, with Prem Prakash's advice and help, the house was sold to a genuine purchaser with money coming in promptly. Prem

Prakash, this time, was at the forefront from the very beginning. His emphasis all along was on purchaser being good people and accommodating, the sale price settled might be a little less.

Everything proceeded smoothly. They left their old house and shifted to the new one. Now the young guru desired that 'Grih-Pravesh' – the house-warming party – should be organised in a grand way. Prem Prakash was, however, not in favour. He felt that already they had incurred loss in terms of interest having been paid to the first party; over and above, now the expenditure on entertaining a thousand people! It could be avoided. A simple short puja should suffice. He advised the young guru a couple of times but he kept smiling. For him, 'Grih-Pravesh' was going to be an occasion when he will be the centre of attraction, that too as a swamy, a guru. His earlier disciples would be impressed, new ones added. Openly he didn't express his disagreement with Prem Prakash but the smile locked in his round face appeared to say – 'Prem Prakash ji, you, after all, are an outsider. Why are you interfering in our domestic affairs. It is our money which is going to be spent, we are not asking you to provide'. Prem Prakash quietly withdrew, date of 'Grih-Pravesh' got fixed. On the side-lines, she suffered in the tussle. The whole thing might have dissipated in formalities had the young guru gone himself to give the invitation card to Prem Prakash, who had expressed his reservations to him and not to her. The young guru was, however, adept in passing on the buck – "you go, he is your 'sir'." Meant that she should go to put salt on the wound, to convey to Prem Prakash that they didn't go by his advice this time because the money which was being spent was theirs and not his. She had to go, though she didn't want to. Anyway, it was better than the invitation card not reaching Prem Prakash at all.

Prem Prakash was alone in his study.

"I know this is not of your liking but..." she said.

"My liking or me... do not matter, I know."

It was obvious from his facial expression, words spoken, tone thereof that Prem Prakash was hurt – that the job done and he had been thrown out like a fly from the milk-pot.

"You know I am not a party to this celebration," she further said.

"You have come to invite all the same."

"Any excuse to come to you is good enough for me, to be with you for whatever little time."

"Not necessary that we think alike on all matters. You celebrate 'Grah-Pravesh' Who stops?"

"It is thanks to you that we got this house. How can there be 'Grah-Pravesh' of it without you?"

"It is not correct to think that things happen because of X or Y. Sometimes situations so develop that things get spoiled, then they reshape differently and things improve. The process goes on and people get roasted like insects in between."

"It is people who create situations. Some create the destructive ones, others constructive."

"See, I do not at all feel amiss that you are celebrating. It is your business."

"When the sale of the old house was in a mess... then also it was our business."

"The matter was different then... something untoward could have happened. Nothing of the kind is involved in this celebration, only some money... so you people may go ahead."

"I refuse to be included in 'you people'."

"You have to be, you are placed with them."

"I know, but I also know how not to participate, even though outwardly participating. This occasion when everyone comes joyfully to eat, I will not eat the whole day, not even during the evening feast, if you do not come. No 'Grih-Pravesh' for me if you are not there."

Putting the card on the table, she just walked away. Prem Prakash also got up. He was looking at her back, which also carried her strict demeanour.

"Listen... o.k., I will come."

Hearing it, her whole being got electrified. She ran back into the embrace of Prem Prakash, her head dropping into his neck. Turmoil and tensions of past so many days and months... breaking into pieces, were falling on Prem Prakash.

She felt as if she had entered a cave... cool and secure. Was she in a somnolent state or half-dead? The world outside, her own being had ceased to exist, only a fragrance emanating from where her cheek lay on Prem Prakash's chest. One hand of Prem Prakash held her in light embrace, the other stroked her back softly."

"My little wounded bird! How have you suffered last few months? I can't see you suffering."

Lifting her head she let her lips slip into those of Prem Prakash.

Prem Prakash reached her house in the evening. The 'Pandal' raised for the feast was empty. Whole day long, people had come intermittently to eat, congratulate or bless. Now came the left-over few, who ate either in the house, verandah or where the foodstuff prepared by the halwai had been kept – puri, vegetables, curd, sweet, etc. Beside the house was a covered space, which they had purchased additionally for the temple. Statue of Devi had not yet been installed but small or middle-sized deities had been seated on the celestial throne of their previous house. Saffron flag flew over the cover of the space to indicate that there would be a temple here. Name-plate outside the house had also been fixed – her husband's name prefixed by 'Swami' and suffixed by 'Anand'. No mention of the father-in-law, whose house had been sold to purchase this one; she was a non-entity anyway, though the father-in-law had purchased the house in the joint names of his son and daughter-in-law.

The moment she saw Prem Prakash, she was thrilled. Her face fatigued with day's long work suddenly blossomed up.

She was in sari-blouse. Prem Prakash was seeing her in this dress for the second time. First time, when they had only recently known each other and she had come to his house. Prem Prakash had burst into laughter – she appeared to have been wrapped into a bedsheet! Sari doesn't befit ladies of slender frame – he then thought. On her part, she was almost moved to tears and even complained mildly to Prem Prakash's wife – "Sir is making fun of me!" Today she looked beautiful in yellow sari and red blouse. Her face was reddish but the colour of lips had faded, she had not used lipstick, the wind... fatigue or tension, maybe. She had put plentiful of vermilion in the parting of the hair. Prem Prakash found it strange. A lady who was almost fed up with her husband, despised him... she holds her marital status in such high esteem, as to prominently displaying it? He could never understand this peculiar tendency of Indian women. She doesn't believe in keeping up appearances, why this show off!

She rushed to him as if had been waiting only for him, the whole day long. Unconscious of people around, she took Prem Prakash by hand – 'Come, I show you the house' – carried him to the stairs straight for upper portion of the house, skipping the ground floor. She walked very close, almost clasping him.

She didn't say a word about the big room upstairs which they entered first and which was obviously their bedroom; she was just not interested in it. Hurriedly leading Prem Prakash through it, she took him to the small roof that lay beside and said – "I will sit in the evening here beneath the stars and day time under the sun... to fondly think about whomsoever I wish to..."

She stopped. Some people from the ground floor had come up, accompanied by her mother-in-law. Throwing a formal smile at them, she took Prem Prakash to the side-room.

"This is mother-in-law's room, bathroom is attached. Let us go to the top floor."

Circular iron stair-case led them to the roof at the top. There were hills on the left, no multi-storeyed building had come up so far.

'What should I be doing here?' She asked.

"Drying up the washed clothes... and your hair," Prem Prakash replied.

"Don't make fun, please tell me."

"Sit quietly here... watching the hills."

"These bald hillocks?"

"Yes, they didn't get anything from the world – we got something anyway – yet they stand, detached, though seeing everything!"

"Human beings can't be that detached? Hills are stones after all."

"As per mythology, there was a time when they had feathers, could fly. A time came when they became immobile. shows it doesn't pay to be very mobile. In our mythology, there is a story about Goverdhan or Vindhyachal mountain – a saint cursed the mountain – 'stay put'. It became static. Nonetheless staying capacity can be imbibed from them. To stay on... as in this house you may."

"I don't want to... living in the heart of a person whom you love – that is understandable. I would only learn detachment from these hills."

They came down. The ground floor had the kitchen, a room (earmarked for the father-in-law probably), a bath and a hall. On one side lay material used in the puja, already performed; pictures of the deities, statues had been put against the wall. She made Prem Prakash sit there and herself sat down close by. Off and on under everyone's gaze, she would in a very natural way put her hand on Prem Prakash's ankle. Prem Prakash felt a little awkward, but she was not bothered, even continued drawing herself closer and closer to him.

She, it seems, is announcing to the whole world – 'look, what he is to me, no one else is.' I appreciate her feelings... but why should they be announced? Their piety lies in the fact that they are confined to two and a curtain is drawn for the outer world. Probably, what is involved here for her is not our feelings. She feels proud of me and she definitely wants to tell her family members, if not the whole world, that this is the person with whose help we are sitting here in this house and it is she who discovered him. But this precisely is what is dangerous and she doesn't understand it, doesn't care probably. If she does, maybe it is her overzealousness oozing out—that she brought me here.

"Just coming. Be here...," suddenly she got up and went upstairs to check whether Prem Prakash could dine there. People were still passing through.

She returned, slightly ill at ease. Then headed straight to the place where food-stuff was stored and started putting food items in a thali. Meanwhile, finding Prem Prakash alone, the young guru came over and sat beside him. She came from behind and told him, "Some guests have gone to the temple side, you go and attend them. I shall serve food to sir."

The young guru rushed to the temple-side. She put the thali before Prem Prakash on the dari and sat down close to him as before.

Suddenly, power went off and it was darkness all over. Prem Prakash thought he would commence eating only after the lights returned... but just then he felt the touch of tender fingers – slightly shaking – on his lips. The fingers slipped a morsel of puri and vegetables in Prem Prakash's mouth and withdrew. The touch of her trembling fingers left Prem Prakash's lips burning. He awaited a repeat... but power returned. In her fingers was ready another morsel which she quickly put in her own mouth.

Smilingly she was looking at Prem Prakash.

Prem Prakash started eating. Shortly she got up to be with other guests. After finishing food, Prem Prakash thought of leaving. He hardly ever attended such functions or marriage. When he did as he must, he immediately started thinking of how to get out as early as possible.

If essentially life is sad, to celebrate happiness crying hoarse, sounds strange to me. As if birthdays, marriages, grih-pravesh, etc. do not happen to others. Inhabitants of this house are running about here and there... upbeat in joy, parading affinity for each other, she too, while inside they carry suppressed miseries, animosities towards each other.

She in the midst of people, surrounded by them is presently the focal point, so is very happy. How many contradictions are there in her – indifferent to family and home, yet domestic, happy about 'Grih-pravesh'; enemical to marriage, yet proudly displaying her marital status – despite having bob-cut, she so combed her hair as to carve out the middle line – '*maang*', rather than letting the bob-cut flow free; instead of giving just a touch of it,

she poured plenty of vermilion in the maang, so much so that it is now spreading all over her hair. She wants to be happy, has the capacity to pull happiness to her-fed me with her hands in such a crowd!

Reaching her, Prem Prakash asked from behind – 'May I leave?'. She, aggrieved like a child, said, "No, not right now. You have only just arrived. Join you in a minute."

Prem Prakash returned to his place. She did come forthwith but couldn't stay with him for long; she had to go out again to greet this guest or the other. After a while, Prem Prakash again asked to leave. This time she did not refuse – was, however, sad, little angry too. She didn't come out to see him off as Prem Prakash did whenever she came to his house.

Next day she complained on phone – 'Couldn't you stay a little longer?'

She has it in her to sort of pull happiness to her but can't hold on to it for long. Why couldn't she be happy for the next few days just for this – that I, after all, did attend her 'Grih-Pravesh'. Although I do not go out for such functions, yet I went, for her sake only. But soon after, she was unhappy, little angry too that I didn't stay longer. Had I, what would she have done of me, had already fed me. Probably, she wanted me to be just there, whether she was able to be with me or not. Just my presence – to make her feel that I was part of her house.

She pulled unhappiness to her the same way as the happiness of feeding me with her hands.

What is she after all? I have read numerous books of psychology, sociology, am experienced too... yet unable to comprehend a girl!

After the 'Grih-pravesh', the young guru let the residential portion of the house remain as it was purchased, but spent a lot on construction of the temple. In the old house also, the temple portion was always more decorated and glamorous than the residential. In the new set-up, the temple was a separate wing... almost another house. It had a separate independent entrance, which led straight to the sanctum, the celestial seat. The common folk may pay obeisance unobstructed and return from this point comfortably. Erecting a wall in the middle, an altogether separate portion within the temple was carved out. There was a small gate in the wall, leading to the waiting room. Further inside was guru's chamber, having his gaddi as in the old house. A bed for Guruji's rest was a new addition here. Visitors sat on the floor as in the old house. The chamber had a wall-to-wall red carpet and was air-conditioned. Doors to the waiting room and chamber – both had automatic door-closers. While the sanctum looked ordinary, this side had an air of luxury about it.

The young guru received visitors in accordance with their position or status. Adult ladies of the neighbourhood were frequent visitors. The young guru devoted more time with the good-looking and the moneyed, tried to establish rapport with them. But those ladies were a clever lot – interested only in killing their free time. Neither young guru's coaxing moved them nor were they seen to be financially helping. They came, talked business and went away. All the same, how much time had to be given to whom – was decided by the young guru. No assistant, because it would violate privacy. Entry in this exclusive portion was prohibited even for his favourite pupils. Guru met them outside in the sanctum or at his residence. When no visitors, Guru was alone inside, said to be busy meditating, reading scriptures or praying.

Young females came accompanied by their parents or friends, but the arrangement set up by guru was such that each individual would as far as possible see him alone, tell his/her problems in private. Even in the matter involving a couple, husband and wife were to see him separately. Even if the adult ladies came in a flock, they had to see the young guru individually, a must in their second visit.

That night, after the 'aarti, there were only three visitors, who insisted on being heard together as the matter was common to them. Parents and their daughter – problem of her marriage. They had come with her horoscope to know about the likely time of her marriage.

Taking the horoscope, the young guru looked at them one by one, daughter more closely. Young, wheatish complexion, which successfully suppressed mild traces of small-pox in childhood, big eyes.

Freshness of early youth. Being short, her figure appeared to be more fleshy than of her age.

"What's the name of the blessed one?"

'Nisha' – replied the father.

"Good name. Nisha – night, to give rest. If night were not there, people will not be able to rest, will go mad."

"We have brought her along because you see both the horoscope and the hand."

"Both are complimentary to each other. What is indicated by one is confirmed by another – leading us to conclude that our assessment is correct after all. What's the problem?"

"Proposals of her marriage get broken half-way on some very ordinary, sometimes silly pretexts."

Young guru glanced through the horoscope for a while, counted something on his pores, then said "Nisha, Come close, my dear."

Nisha pulled herself close to gaddi. The young guru took her left hand in his, felt the trembling of the fresh leaf. He scanned the lines. In the process of opening and closing the palm from here and there, he affectionately pressed it too – so tender, so beautiful. He devoted more time in reading the hand than the horoscope. While he looked at her face – face reading – he held the beautiful hand. Finally when he let it go, he was little restless, speechless and grave outside.

"What does the guruji say?"

"Dim... very dim?"

"You mean, marriage is not indicated at all?"

"Not that. Caught by three opposite planets for three years. If fixed or performed in spite of that, any mishap may happen."

Again he took the horoscope. Studying and counting, he further said – "After three years, 'Mahadasha of guru (Vrhispati) enters. Think about her marriage only then. Until then let her wear ring with neelam in it, fast and worship to appease the planets that are opposed."

The parents looked worried, so the young guru teased them in a light vein – 'Why are you in a hurry to throw her out?'

"She has completed her B.A, idling at home… getting older for marriage...

"These days it is no age. The problem of staying at home, of course, is there. Let her study further."

"She doesn't have much appetite for that."

"Will develop... I will introduce her to my wife, who is very sharp in studies. We both, after talking to this young thing, shall find out a subject which interests her. My wife knows people in the university; she will get her admitted there, her appetite for studies shall grow. Nisha, you come tomorrow afternoon – not here to my residence. If I am not there, my wife would be there... be with her. Three of us would plan for your future."

"What about neelam?" The father was still worried.

"You get a ring for her finger. I will get pure neelam. Whatever fasts, worshipping have to be done by Nisha, I would eventually explain to her.

The young guru got up.

Nisha came the next day. Young guru has already briefed his wife. She didn't like the idea of anyone exploiting her contacts but on learning that further studies of a female are at stake, she felt pity for Nisha and agreed. The trio decided that Nisha do Masters in history. Right then, before Nisha, she talked to the Reader in her earlier Department. Nisha had to meet him in a couple of days; he would take her to the history department, where all the formalities shall be completed.

There only the young guru explained to her the fasts, which Nisha had to do every Monday and Saturday. While he was explaining the methodology, his wife left them.

The young guru came out to see Nisha off, noticed that she was without a scooter, had come by bus.

"I will drop you home. Where is it?"

Nisha told him the locality but immediately added –

"I shall take the bus; there is a direct one."

"What difference does it make. I have to go that side only."

"Just now?"

"Yes. Come on. It's on my way. Shall meet your parents too."

Nisha's father didn't keep well, was due to retire in a couple of months, so naturally was worried about Nisha's marriage. She was his only issue. Unfortunately, Nisha was ordinary to look at, which caused hurdles for the marriage. Demand of dowry spoiled, when talks made a little headway. To improve his financial state, Nisha's father was constructing a small residential unit on the roof of his house. Rent would be an additional source of income after retirement.

The young guru talked very sweetly. He won over the parents of Nisha, the same day. On the day fixed, he took Nisha to the university in his scooter, got all formalities of admission completed.

He frequently phoned them now, talked mostly to Nisha's father. Gradually, he started sharing the errands connected with the construction on the roof – going to the market, ordering material, discussing with the contractor, etc. Nisha's father couldn't do that much running about, so it was a big relief to him. At times, it was required to stand on the roof under the sun to oversee work like putting up the slab, etc. – the young guru took it upon himself. He went over to their house day time and sometimes was there the whole day. On such occasions, Nisha would cook something, make tea for him – the young guru felt elated.

In course of only a few days, he had become quite intimate, almost a part of the family. Whenever he chanced to be alone with Nisha, he would tell her about astrology. Nisha was getting more interested in it than in history, her subject.

"Can you teach me astrology?" One day she asked him.

"But you are studying history."

"That doesn't engage me fully. I can do something over and above."

"All right, but the student has to come to the teacher..." – the young guru said coquettishly. Nisha looked in askance, so he put it straight – "For that, you will have to come to me. One hour a week should suffice. We will study in the drawing room."

"I shall come. It's only half-an-hour by bus to your house."

"Ask your father."

"He won't object. He is more enthusiastic than me in matters of study."

Her father immediately agreed. If in addition to her M.A, his daughter is able to learn one more subject, all the better. Besides, she will be busy.

The young guru taught in the drawing room only twice – at a time when his wife was away on job. Third time he suggested – "Let us sit in the temple. There is disturbance here."

They started sitting in the inner apartment of the temple – where Nisha had come initially. Daytime it was quiet on the temple side. The day when Nisha were to come, the young guru returned from his office early. He had studied astrology for a degree. He followed the same gradual sequence in teaching Nisha. Simultaneously proceeded the other sequence – touching, teasing, moving up to clasping and kissing. That far Nisha didn't object – he had after all become part of the house, shared her father's anxiety and effort in so many matters, stood like a wall of support to them. Moreover, it was a new pleasure Nisha was gradually being introduced to. The young guru was fair-complexioned, good to look at and they were almost of the same age. When the young guru took the next step, Nisha objected –

"Not this."

"Why?"

"Not here."

"Why?"

"Someone would see."

"No one comes here."

"Didi – your wife?"

"She is in her office."

"Parents?"

"They are usually at home at this hour. Today, they too have gone out."

"Not now."

The young guru didn't press. She will have to be prepared mentally. When both sat down as before, Nisha asked –

"You are married. Is it not infidelity to your wife?"

"I don't love her."

"Why?"

"We don't think alike. She had no interest in religious activities. How much am I involved, you have seen for yourself. She insults religion, me, God. We took Deeksha together. She took part in religious ceremonies initially, then stopped for no reason. Is it not infidelity? Since then, we are on different paths."

"Does your religion permit adultery?"

"I love you, so it is not irreligious."

"Is it not an impendiment – you being a priest."

"A priest is also a human being. I have not forsaken the world."

"Why love for me?"

"Because our interests are alike. You have interest in astrology... my field. You worship, you fast... as I tell you. You care for me. We think of each other's future. I like you very much... and why should you vegetate until marriage? Youth and the present shall vanish fast... should not be wasted. Modern girls experience all this before marriage... it is prevalent now."

Nisha was beginning to get acquainted with the pleasures of flesh her university friends talked about with relish.

The sequence had commenced. As soon as they were alone, they fell upon each other as the time or the situation permitted. Parents of Nisha were assured that the young guru was a religious man, married. In the house, there were young guru's parents and son besides his wife. They had become accustomed to see Nisha sitting at the back of young guru's scooter.

The young guru now saved money to buy some gift for Nisha – some dress or ornaments not very costly. Nisha would either not disclose it at home or explain it away as having been given in the university by a female friend.

Parents of Nisha were slightly anxious about defamation... but Nisha went out daytime only – that too mostly to the university.

The young guru waited for her there; she bunked the classes and they would go anywhere... or the temple apartment, bypassing the residence. Study of astrology was no longer confined to a day in the week.

The young guru was not bothered about his parents, or his wife for that matter. His worry was his disciples— who were wayward but also carriers of his prestige. Luckily, they didn't come this side during the day, when the guru, they thought, would be in his office. Most of them slept daytime.

"We seldom go out together. He would go with sandlewood paste on his forehead; dressed all red, heavy bead necklaces, rings studded with auspicious stones on his fluffy fingers. Thinks that this way he looks out of the ordinary, influential but is it necessary to appear thus all the time before all the people? Can we not go sometimes casually as others do, just to meet people; everywhere this yellow tilak and red robe? He wants to show off – that he has taken deeksha, is extraordinary. These things should be confined to the temple while worshiping or at best when you are meeting the devotees. Twenty-four hours? He keeps small hair, so that his forehead may look broad with tilak pasted from this end to that – swami, only swami and swami all the way, the human not allowed to be visible from any corner.

We got married in quite a filmy style. We were in the same town. I was studying in twelfth class, used to go to the college cycling. One day he collided against me in such a way that my bicycle comes over his. An ordinary student, acting as a bollywood hero! At the very first sight, I detested him, his method. I mentioned this to my step brothers, who gave him a good thrashing. He complained to the police, bribed them with money taken from his parents. The police-walas would now harass my brothers. Then one day, closeting me alone, he threatened – 'I will stab myself before you, if you do not say yes. Will marry you, else commit suicide.' Filmy style again! I got alarmed, was confused too. Hated him all the more.

My parents were no more. Had only step-mother with whom I shared. She worried more on account of her sons than for me.

She said – 'you have to get married in any case, with this man or that. All men are the same after marriage. This man would do only what others will; the man you choose would also do the same. Good that we had not to go searching, the boy himself turned up. He is young, studying, loves you. What else would you seek? Okay it, put only one condition – that he withdraws the complaint made against your brothers. Police harass them like anything; poor things! they fear to get out of the house'.

My step-mother never treated me well. After that incident, she stopped my going to the college. Same old argument—girls are not required to study, they should only learn to do domestic chores – which you have to do all your life. If you had to study, why were you born a female? Until now you are not defaced, so someone would marry you. If your face gets disfigured in course of quarrels and fight, no one would marry you, then you shall be on me all your life! Bloody, have you taken birth to be a life-burden on me?" I thought – I was not going to get anything in my step mother's house, because I was a girl – which was my biggest crime. Something better might turn up in the new house – so I said yes to this man. I put two conditions before him – withdraw complaint against my brothers and my studies should not be discontinued. He, being mad after me, agreed. Full marks to him that he complied with both... but what about the extra which he kept on doing simultaneously?"

Prem Prakash saw that her eyes had got watery. Deepening shadows of big trees in the park had darkened her face. Obviously, she very much desired a happy marital life to immerse in... but that was not to be. She went on –

"After marriage, he took 'deeksha', coerced me also to do the same. If you were so much inclined, why did you not take it before marriage and why marriage at all... I questioned. His reply was – 'it is pleasure to work together. Both of us would do religious work, spread Guruji's message, while remaining householders at the same time. We would worship, observe fast, etc., hold ceremonies together as a couple as Guruji dictates.'

Was this the only area to go together? No thought as to what the other person wished? He would make me sit beside him as guruain (priestess) on even trifle occasion. Got the twin satisfaction of being a guru and me sitting by his side. The ire suppressed inside me went on piling up and started coming out. Now each time I objected, sometimes would sit on the 'chauki' crying. People watched all this, he felt his prestige affected. Eventually, he started escorting me only after preparing me mentally for each occasion. Even then my soul rebelled – doing that I don't have faith in, which is hypocritical... sitting with the man in red – colour which I hate. Why should I sit with him in functions, said to be spiritual, where my spirit rebelled. One day I refused point-blank. I now keep myself away from the temple.

I wanted to do science. Studied B.Sc. for one year in a college; his parents couldn't stomach it. Mother-in-law – a mother-in-law after all – started complaining – 'Are we to sit like this only, did we marry our son for this, what do we do the whole day long, we also need a toy to play with'.

I wanted to appear in the Pre-medical competitive exam, aspired to be a doctor – was very good in studies till twelfth... but this man prevailed upon me. Siddartha was born those days only. They wanted a toy but everyone excused himself/herself when it came to looking after. I used to keep awake whole night and rush to the college in the morning. Couldn't cope so this man suggested that I switch over to B.A, it would be lighter. My mother-in-law had asked for a toy but... till the other day, when I had to go to Harbhajan for the case, my in-laws would push Siddartha behind. The poor thing, feeling sleepy sitting there without food till 12 in the night! My in-laws would just not keep him – a toy they wanted to play with! No pity for the little thing and you know, in the matter of sale of the house, negative role of my father-in-law was not any less than that of my husband, the spoiler. But he kept on saying – the new house was being purchased in the names of both of you; it was for you to be alert. This is what they are – outwardly simple, cruel inside.

It's not a new phenomenon. Mother-in-law wanted her son to marry only me – do you know why? Of course, any mother desires to do the liking of her son but it was also revenge. She wanted the girl to be in her house permanently, so that she could perpetrate all kinds of cruelties on her to take revenge, punish all her life. Else tell me – which mother would like to marry her son with a girl whose brothers thrashed him."

"But I don't see any big cruelty in your mother-in-law. She may be growling inside, her face too appears to be drawn and cruel but in her behaviour with you..."

"That's what she shows. She is also scared. I told you that very often she taunts me saying – 'the blighter knows that our finger is under the wheel'."

Do you know what that means? The lady who came in this house before me was tortured like anything by my mother-in-law."

"You mean, it is second marriage?"

"No, my father-in-law had no issue for quite a long time. So, he had adopted a son who loved his wife. My mother-in-law taunted and abused her left and right, day in day out. Always looked at her with anger, turned out all the maid-servants and made her do their work. Sometimes, she also gave the poor thing a beating. Fed up, they both committed suicide."

Prem Prakash got panicky. A tragedy of this purport... not reflected on the face of any member of the family including she – who talked about it only now. It was an average middle-class family but what terrible things it had gone through. That tragedy passed off, but its shadow must be lingering over this house, on all of them. How could they stay normal under that shadow!

And how could she!

Suddenly, Prem Prakash got scared of her. He stared at her... looking for any reflection of that tragedy in her face, any shadow of it. The incident would have occurred in the old house, where Prem Prakash had been a number of times. Maybe, they sold it off for that reason.

"Did you see them?"

"No, it happened earlier."

"In your old house?"

"No, in the old town... where both our families resided once. Father-in-law was posted there. It became a police-case, got somehow suppressed by father-in-law. He loved his adopted son. Satyendra was his name, he called him – Baré, the elder one. Once the case got suppressed, father-in-law out of fright took retirement and shifted over here."

"You lived in that house?"

"Yes, for little less than a year."

"Your mother must be knowing all about this."

"It was a small town, all seniors knew."

"Despite knowledge about that incident in the family, she gave you in marriage?"

"I told you she wanted to get rid of me."

"You didn't feel scared?"

"I learnt about the incident after my marriage. The room where both committed suicide was kept locked. For some days, while passing by, I did feel scared... eventually got used. Inside me, something hard was brewing – that eventually I have also to go the way she went, the earlier one. Mother-in-law habitually acted tough on me... that time both she and me looked towards that room which was her past and my future!

How did she look – the one who passed away? Was she alike – beautiful, tender, sensitive like the one before me – burnt out by the wrath of the mother-in-law, another woman? Newspapers abound with such incidents... but then you don't feel much. Today, as if the incident was happening before me. She, was the mirror – the incident casting its shadow direct on her face, which reflected it. Dark shadow – she is aware that mother-in-law's behaviour towards her might be a little changed, but she, her second daughter in-law is bound to go the way the first one has gone. It is destined, she can't escape it. Her face has hardened, unflutterd she is just gazing – yes, she can't escape. Desire to live has already gone.

"I feel enraged with your mother – you don't throw your daughter in a family which has this kind of history!"

"You will have to try hard to appreciate that in our country, there are several such places, homes and families where a girl is nothing more than dirt; makes no difference whether she lives or dies.

"Husband's behaviour with you immediately after marriage at least must have been good."

"Master daytime, butcher at night – has been the pattern from the very beginning. For him, that's what a husband should be. He never paused to think that I could also wish, desire. Took it for granted that whatever was his desire shall be mine too, has to be. 'All right, now you do B.A... now study private, have to look after the child... your mother had decided not to educate you after twelfth, should feel indebted to me that you are post-graduate...' talks like this. Being a husband, he feels that he has unlimited rights over me. Doesn't beat... but mental torture inflicted is more serious. To hurt in diverse ways, speak tauntingly, do with me whatever and whenever... because he is husband; not only he himself insults me, gets me insulted by others too. Left me alone at Harbhajan's. Once Harbhajan poured gutka in my mouth saying Bhabhi-Bhabhi... I vomited like anything on the way, had to halt in my friend's house. Instead of feeling enraged at Harbhajan, this man just laughed. When I pointed that it was an insult to his wife, he simply said – 'we are under duress, Harbhajan may not do our work if he felt amiss.' Bloody if Harbhajan won't, are there no other lawyers in the town? Tomorrow you will send your wife to sleep with him in order to keep him in good humour!"

Her eyes were aflame, face reflected hatred towards world entire. Insults for being a female child at mother's house, for a daughter-in-law in inlaws'; insult by the husband, by others through the husband... insults every step! She was sitting as it were, on heap of dry hay, which could catch fire any moment with a spark of her anger.

"Do you know, I am scared to go out with him – don't know which situation he may put you in. Wife with her husband feels secure... conversely I feel insecure whenever with him alone. As for him, he would just giggle in whatever situation."

Circles which form around her, inside out, are each more painful than the preceding – from real to the step-mother; thrown over to the inlaws... might be better in some respects, but more torture here; did not have father's security, should have got husband's at least. How was she saved at all... when all stuff there was to drive her in the direction taken by the first one, could commit suicide alone. What kept her alive, still keeping?

"You are the first with whom I could share all this. With others, I only have to smile. They think – everything is here—husband, own house, a son, father-in-law for protection, mother-in-law to share domestic chores... and now, with your help, I have employment too."

She smiled... thick layer of sadness underneath. It was neither self-pity, nor any kind of persecution-mania – that all are out to torture her. Evil people and circumstances frequent everyone's life... but here they had come to stay.

"You don't see anything good in your family members?"

"Why not? Husband, for instance, is pious, doesn't touch non-veg, drink or smoke, doesn't beat me... but is a despot. Father-in-law is very kind – would contemplate bringing home any hurt cub or chick he comes across, but no pity for a human being brought home, i.e., me. Mother-in-law, is an excellent cook but would not enter the kitchen lest it should give me relief, takes great care of his daughter... but can't treat me as her daughter. Unfortunately, from the very beginning, circumstances so shaped that all three of them were enemical towards me, their weaknesses adding fuel to the fire."

"Is there no remedy?"

"Remedy? Nothing. I am not responsible for the circumstances or their nature for that matter. What is there in my hands except my own self?" A deep sigh followed.

The point where helplessness is of that order that recounting our pain or sorrows itself looks frivolous! Go on living silently, bearing whatever life brings. It was what she had been doing. I provoked and she started thinking. Now she looks towards me – that I may probably show her the way... and I get scared. Is there a way at all? What could I do with my life? Putting aside circumstances and people, clung to the activity of reading, writing, convinced that whatever I would get, it would be from my work only. In a way ran away... thus washed off. The poor lady can't even run away, is destined to live like a prisoner in that house. Little change for her in service – during service hours only, there too with the constant feeling that you have ultimately to return to your house only.

Deepening shadows below the trees were inching towards them. There were no flowers on plants around. The grass was dry and dull, crushed at places. Chirping of birds had commenced on one or two dense trees near about. The birds sat on one for some time, then flew to another – quest for the night-shelter!

Darkness descended. They got up to leave. While returning, Prem Prakash drew her close, her head fell into his neck... as a chick into the security of the nest.

Prem Prakash felt remorse – why did he provoke her to say, to go through all that again. What's the point?

He patted her tenderly.

She thought their standard of living shall move up the ladder even though slightly, once salary of two started coming to the house. They would be able to give better upbringing to Siddarth. That's why she always goaded the young guru to search for himself a job which is more paying, but to no effect. If she pestered further, he would say – 'where is the need, your pay is there anyway, take it as my increased salary.' Actually, he had started slackening down since she got employed.

One day she noticed that the young guru was not going to his office for past several days, had been loitering in the house only. Came to know that he has been suspended. This was bound to happen because he frequently absented himself from the office on one pretext or the other – doesn't feel like going today, is on navratri fast, or Ganapati has been installed. He thought he was engaged in something big... much bigger than the job; the employers should appreciate. Our country having religious festivals every week, how long would any employer put up with it... a private one at that? She advised – 'nothing is lost yet, go and apologise, promise that it would not happen in future, won't be on leave like this, would be responsible and disciplined.' He retorted – "Why should I go? Let them call; if they do, I shall think about it."

Bravo! Is there any dearth of service-aspirants in the country that an employer would sit waiting for him only, implore him as if he is blessed with feathers of flamingoes or is some specialist indispensable, that work of the employer will simply stop without him?

"Why should I labour there for a trifle..." he further said.

The young guru had taken loan from his office. Salary was bound to be reduced after deduction of the instalment of repayment. He had not thought about it while borrowing. Now since he was not getting full pay, he had lost interest in the job. When she raised the issue as to how will the house run, he shouted back – "How are you concerned! I may bring money from wherever. Besides, father's pension is there."

She doesn't like being dependent on father-in-law. As it is they are residing in his house, he also spends on the household out of his pension. To be entirely dependent on him, on old people... when ours is the age to work, earn – this was not palatable to her.

"I just don't feel like doing a job – that is it. I want to give full time to religious activities. You are earning in any case."

He finished the topic, didn't go back to his office to apologise or to work. Actually, he didn't want to do any job, because it inconvenienced him to meet, be with Nisha. Now whole day was at his disposal, he could meet whenever it suited her. As for his son's future – anyway he would inherit this house with all necessary accessories, he doesn't have to struggle for them; if the boy doesn't get any job, the temple is there to engage him. If the young guru can keep himself engaged – worshipping, counseling, preaching – his son can also do the same.

The money borrowed from office was adjusted against his provident fund accumulation. The young guru didn't go to his office even for settling his final accounts. Letter of termination reached his house, along with the cheque for the little residual amount.

For her, it brought an additional discomfort. What would she now say if someone were to ask – what does your husband do. If someone asked Siddarth about his father's occupation, what would the poor boy say – that he worships, sits in the home-temple?

One night in slumber, she felt something creeping over her legs upwards, spitting all the way, leaving dirty liquid behind, some filthy dampness. She tried to throw it away from one place, it moved to another... disgusting.

Siddarth was sleeping by her side. She always made him sleep in the middle, between her and the young guru. Taking advantage of the darkness and the fact that Siddarth was fast asleep, the young guru had stealthily moved over to her side. Kissing her legs, then the thighs... he was now trying to slip her gown upwards, could come upon her anytime. Collecting her full strength, she gave a big kick to guru, towards the leg-side of the bed. The young guru fell down. She got up in panic with a nauseating feeling, ran straight to the bathroom, locked it from inside and sitting on the floor vomited... didn't have the strength to stand before the wash-basin, having spent whole of it in pushing away the young guru.

Out of bathroom, she headed to the open terrace, started moving to and fro there to unwind.

Row-houses, such as theirs', spread from this end to that in L-shape, lay asleep, lifeless under the dim light of the stars. For the first time, she noticed that in the entire campus, there was not a single tree. It was concrete jungle – this corner to that. Capping the houses there were only hills – bald hills.

"Watch them from here,"... Prem Prakash had said. Would she be able to, if so, for how long? Trees over there had already vanished, some day the hills would vanish too, that area would also turn into a concrete jungle.

In-law's house... she has been giving much more than she took. Her salary – whole of it. Over and above doing the domestic chores – cooking for the entire family, washing clothes of self, husband and son, cleaning utensils and the house if the maid doesn't turn up. Numerous chores associated with husband – washing his clothes including undergarments, temple attire, which she detests, press them after wash. The young guru in for bath, she, towel in hand, standing at the doorstep to hand over the towel, when he calls for it. In course of it sometime, the young guru would pull her inside the bathroom, force himself on her; she let him, up to the tolerable limit. Bringing out the clothes guru has to wear after bath. The young guru would eat only the stuff cooked by his wife, who should also sit across while he is eating, continue sitting there; she not there, he would push away the arranged thali, get up without eating. If he were to go out of town, wife should get the suitcase done. He would just pick it up and march. Wife has to imagine things he would require in a particular town; if something found missing there, she has to face the music.

And what did he do... her husband? A job – whatever it was – given up. He must have all the rights of a husband, particularly over her body in whatever manner it pleases him and whenever, she inclined or not!

His desire alone! Her soul rebels. Whenever he touches her amorously, she feels as if she is being dragged to sit on the pyre alive.

That which makes her soul rebel – she simply won't do now. She won't let her be the object of his passion, to be enjoyed whenever desired. She is not some eatable stuff that you put it in your mouth, whenever. Why should she give herself to a man for whom she doesn't feel, who doesn't care for her self-respect, doesn't provide security that a wife needs, doesn't earn? Why should she allow violent pricking on her body... just because he became her husband taking advantage of her helplessness, her adverse circumstances?

This body – it is hers. This is the only thing she got when born, only thing she can call her own. Inside it only reside the soul, heart... whatever. This is the temple of her being. She won't let it be maligned with punk, permit anyone to tear it apart – not even her husband. She detests sex... which caused Siddarth's birth. Whenever she looks at him, she is overpowered with guilt – his parents not doing enough for his upbringing, don't provide proper atmosphere for it; what would he be, when he grows up –

only a hypocrite, worshipping in this very temple, like his father!

Her spontaneous reaction just now to her husband's advances... she would clothe it in a resolution, will put it in practice, soberly, of course. If the young guru doesn't take the hint even then, she may put it to him bluntly.

In exchange what shall she forsake?

She would not beg any money from this so-called husband, even if it is related to her education. Shall certainly ask out of her salary – as a matter of right.

Husband got her educated, she also gave herself in all possible ways in return. The deal gets over here. Quits!

Thus far and no further.

Work related to her Ph.D. was over. She had submitted her thesis.

She was in girl's college for her B.A and M.A. There she suffered from inferiority complex that almost all her classmates – some elder to her – were unmarried, life was to open up for them and here she was – married, mother of a child! In M.Phil., it was co-ed but students in the class were few. Dr. Kaushik was in-charge. Lean and thin, he could be sighted anytime puffing his cigarette outside the department. Always in tension. Composed poetry. Had got a couple of books of his poems published, but few knew him as a poet outside the campus, nor was it his goal. All which he aspired was that in the crowd of university students and teachers, he should also be known for something, over and above a teacher. Additional regard.

Very often after the classes, Prof. Kaushik called her in his chamber and made her sit till the department emptied. Then his fingers, on some pretext, started crawling wrist upwards... and she, very cleverly diverting Professor's mind somehow sneaked out. Couldn't rebel, had to come in his contact everyday, take his guidance, get from him books not available in the university library. Besides, in the finals, he as the internal examiner was a must for one paper as well as for the viva voce. So, she tried to keep him in good humour, brushing aside his objectionable behaviour at times. She would start looking for some pretext or the other to slip away the moment Professor called her in his chamber; quite often she left the department, bunking the last period or rushed to her scooty minutes before it was to be over—so that she remained out of his sight as far as possible. Sometimes on some holiday Prof Kaushik called her home when he was alone; asked her to make tea or cook something in the kitchen. All this while, her heart palpitated, even though she did the errands. One night when after cooking the night meals for the Professor she was about to leave, Professor told her point-blank – "You know I write poetry. I need your help there as you need mine in your studies. I give you intellectual satisfaction, you give me the emotional. You know what I mean?" So, at last, she was driven to the point where she had to take a stand. In such situations, something strange happened to her. Her spine would get erect, eyes aflame. She, however, controlled herself and replied in a very composed way –

"Sir, you know I am married and mother of a child."

"So what! Of what use is your education if you remain caught in that conservative web. I am also married. It makes it convenient.

"Sir, if you say, I can leave the studies."

Without adding a word further, she stepped into her shoes and briskly walked away.

Since then, Professor Kaushik did not call her home. In his chamber too, he called only when he was with people. There to make amends, he tried to give the impression that being a poet, he was by nature sentimental and loving and for that he is often misunderstood. Whenever chanced he would still do some mischief – sometimes touch her arm tenderly, pat her or just lovingly scatter her hair, as if he was doing it as a matter of habit only, was helpless there as in the matter of smoking.

She had got second position only because she had not obliged Professor Kaushik. She knew it, but couldn't open the secret to anyone, not even to Prem Prakash.

In course of registration for her Ph.D. too, Professor Kaushik did not let her go out of his control. If she approached any other Professor to be her guide, he would throw her back to Professor Kaushik. Ultimately, she had to get herself registered only under him. That over, Professor started opening his cards – his fee on every occasion, over and above the university fees. Now he acted professional and dry as was affectionate and caring earlier. It was downright bribery. Sometimes she objected mildly; he would then cite instances of other professors in other departments, emphasising it was customary. If someone said wherefrom the students, without any source of income, raise the money, he would get very rough. 'That was not his problem, let them bring from parents, beg, borrow or steal'. Till her thesis was submitted, she kept fulfilling his demands; the money involved was also not much. Sometimes she took from father-in-law, or husband. That was earlier...

But now...?

When even six months after the submission of her thesis, things didn't look like moving she reminded Professor Kaushik. He put forth the demand of a huge sum giving numerous reasons – only such examiners have to be nominated who are amenable; they have to be paid in advance so that they clear the thesis and not find faults, else they could always ask you to do it all over again; so that they come promptly for viva voce and not defer it repeatedly. Right now they have to be paid return fare of AC two-tier, though that amount is reimbursed to them later on by the university, but it takes time. It is customary, you may check anywhere. Thirdly, they have to be paid for taxi to facilitate their movement in this city. As accommodation is not always available in the university guest-house, you have to pay for the hotel at the rate of ₹ 3000 per day for the day of interview only. The entire sum had to be deposited with Professor Kaushik right in the beginning. On the day of viva voce, he would take her to the examiners to introduce and shall pay them the balance before her. At that time, they will also confirm having received the previous payments.

Total expenditure of around twenty thousand stared at her right now.

These were not the earlier days that she would ask her husband, who could borrow from somewhere, raise the amount. He could still do it, would rather gladly but an unwritten agreement now operated between them; she had asserted herself before him mutely, conveyed it too – he shall not lay claim on her body and she, on her part, shall not demand any money. She could still take it from in-laws but they too belonged to the husband's side. They shall taunt in thousand different ways.

The refuge – Prem Prakash, whom she approached whenever in conflict or turmoil. She raised the issue from the propriety point of view – whether it was proper to pay all this money; was it not bribery?'

"Bribery it certainly is – Prem Prakash said – "but it is also certain that were you not to do all this, your Ph.D. gets held up... maybe for years, the blighters have spread such a network. If you don't pay, your sacrifice alone would not weed out this corruption. The game won't stop by one individual not paying. Right now, many Dr. Kaushiks would be compelling so many students like you to pay. The most horrible aspect of it is that they, who are unemployed, poor, are being compelled to bribe those to whom they have gone far getting educated!

If you don't pay, your labour goes waste. Until you get the degree, your life is stuck up, you can't apply for a proper job. If you proceed to take up arms against this dirt, your life takes a different turn."

"You mean no one should oppose then?"

"One should, but saving one's skin. You have not to offer yourself at the alter."

"If the seniors above are informed?"

"It's not that they do not know, but they are more corrupt than these guys; they have brought these people here. In our days also, these examinations were there but people were different, the entire atmosphere was different."

His head hung in shame, Prem Prakash didn't know what solution to offer to this girl, who was self-respecting. Even if she crosses this hurdle, many more lie ahead. How many would she cross, would fight at how many fronts? Change in the system, in the atmosphere may come, may not... at issue here right now was a life... that stood before him. On her face, red with anger, darkness of frustration was slowly creeping up.

"Do one thing, if you consider it proper. For the time being, handle these cunning people cleverly. First exaggerating your circumstances get the amount reduced, even though slightly. Pay it off and have done with it. When you get your final results, go to thank all of them and then abuse them left and right – that they get guilt-conscious and think of reforming themselves. Even if one changes, we can be satisfied that we did what was due from us in the matter of opposing this malice, succeeded a little bit too... and, of course, you don't be their like later in your life."

She liked this approach and felt relieved instantly. She was an idealist, revolutionary type... at the same time, didn't want that her prospects are affected adversely. Despite overage, she had come so far in her studies that too a hard way—taking obligations, one after another. Each year... each day, it was a battle.

"I have one more problem. I don't have money and I don't want to ask my husband or inlaws. I shall put next month's full pay in it. Can you arrange a loan for me for the residual amount. I shall repay slowly."

"That's not much of a problem. Why ask others, I shall lend you."

Prem Prakash knew that she was not an extracting type. In course of the court case, when he had hinted monetary support to the family, she had come forward daringly to stop other members of the family inclined to accept it. She had so much of self-respect that even here she would have declined, had Prem Prakash offered help. She asked for a loan.

Once the money was arranged, the various stages relating to getting the Ph.D. degree were crossed very fast. She had stopped Professor Kaushik's sexual advances. The frustration got washed off by money he received. Something or the other must come for what he does for a candidate! Where this didn't come about, he felt dull and dry, for he saw it all around, in all areas – people using their power to make underhand money. He happened to be a professor, not having power as such in the job... but had it all the same over beautiful girls, students... must get something for everything he does for them. Colleagues had shown the way. Not only Professor Kaushik's, external examiners' demand was also met. She felt bad that despite she having paid for their stay in the hotel, the examiners' stayed in the university guest-house, where the charges were nominal. As a matter of principle, amount taken from her on this score at least should have been refunded... but they swallowed it. She was in constant touch with Prem Prakash, who always advised her to let the viva voce be over, later on to wait until the results, which came promptly.

She started applying for lectureship as soon as she got her Ph.D., but there too commercialism was in vogue. Private institutions called for the bank-drafts along with the applications and sat over them. Thus, they collected a good sum, earned interest on it and nothing was done to fill up the vacancy which was continued or extension was given to the working employee. The employees were, thus, always kept temporary. A way had been shown by the govt. – don't make even temporary appointments. Appoint on contractual basis, seventy rupees per lecture – labour wage! Lecturers were kept for working days, payments for holidays not required. Appoint in July, dismiss as soon as the college closed or students went on preparation leave. The contractual appointees again running for the job as soon as the colleges reopened. The scheme of contractual appointment had been devised by the state govternment officers, so that their wives, who otherwise had to kill time in kitty parties could get employed. Now jobs were ready for them all the time at all the places where they went on transfer. The officers were unconcerned about the fact that permanent appointments paved the way for a good teaching faculty, which contributed to good education. If education in the country was going to dogs, let it, so long as officers had a hayday.

Owners of private colleges were mostly small-statured political leaders, sychophants or local help of big leaders who rewarded them with the permission to open the colleges, which later on were given recognition or affiliation to the universities. On paper, these colleges were shown to follow university rules, pay as per U.G.C. norms but, in actual practice, it was just the reverse.

Lecturers were given an insignificant amount but were made to sign blank receipts, on which was later on filled the figure prescribed by the U.G.C. Those who objected were shown the door – 'we follow only this system, if you don't like, try another college. Everywhere this was in vogue, where would the Ph.D.s go – at some places, one had to even bribe for getting the employment. She had to remain satisfied with her previous job. That she would get a new one with big salary, once she got Ph.D., remained only a dream, good marks in various examinations hardly ever came out of the marksheets.

"You never ever go to Mayaka, the maternal home?"

After withholding for so many days, when at last she broke the news of young guru having been dismissed from service – Prem Prakash, in order to divert her asked. He didn't wish to get into the mess this time as he had in the matter of the sale of their house. He couldn't do anything about young guru's service anyway.

A sad smile, hollow and short, she turned her face away, looking far at the distance. It seldom happened that she didn't respond to Prem Prakash, who thought she was too involved about her husband's dismissal from services. He wanted to divert her towards something positive. In such unhappy moments, she should think about her parents, her siblings... about her childhood, the games they played then, about her childhood friends... she should get lost in good memories of the past. Face that side, who knows, she might as well be doing just that. Sometimes, it so happens, naturally. That's how we are able to bear sorrow.

Zealously Prem Prakash repeated – "you never ever go to your 'Mayka'."

"I don't have one."

Came the dry retort – prompt and direct, tinged with bitterness. Prem Prakash's lips got sealed. Might be some deep animosity that halted her going to the parents' home, otherwise for a married woman, 'mayka' is such a support. She can rely upon it whenever needed. It is big institution in our social set-up.

Suddenly she turned towards Prem Prakash and said – "Now when you have raised it, know all that too –

My father was a fine human being, very loving towards me. I used to be in small frock then. He lifted me with both hands, threw me up and then caught me in mid-air. Playing with him like this, I giggled a lot, was little scared, being thrown up like that but was also sure that his hands would ultimately catch me up, hold me. Sometimes he would take me on his shoulder to the town end, show me the flock of white birds flying in the sky, going in a certain direction. He wanted to tell me a lot, to make me laugh all the time – for which sometimes he would tickle me too. His only other image that flashes before me is – he has been laid down on the ground, body covered with white sheet, eyes closed, cotton on both nostrils. He who always laughed along with me was lying like this – no movement. I was very small – I didn't understand as to why he is not getting up, as he used to do the moment he saw me. I was told later that a man is said to have died when he is incapable of helping himself. He passed away suddenly – heart attack.

After so many days in the midst of his books, I got some papers, from which I came to know that he was my father indeed but mother was not the one I was living with. Who was my real mother – I never came to know. Hearsay was that while adult and married father fell in love with someone. My brother and I were from her. I was only a few months old when she expired. Then father brought us home.

My step-mother had her own sons, who were very cruel. They would forcibly put me on a tree at such a place that I may not come down. While resisting them, my clothes got torn. I was scared, cried a lot but after putting me there, they would just disappear. I couldn't get down; sometimes for hours, I was on a tree at a desolate place dying with thirst, hunger and fear. Couldn't complain to anyone. After the death of my father, the step-brothers played this cruel joke on me every alternate day. I could get down from the tree only when my real brother came or some passer-by happened to come that way and helped me down. Step-brothers beat me, my real brother tried to shield – in the process, he also got the beating. Father gone, mother's cruelty had increased. She made me do all the domestic chores. Only after giving breakfast to all, could I go to the school. My brother helped in doing the chores. If anything in cooking went wrong, step-mother would punish me – once in Bhindi, I inadvertently put salt twice, the punishment she gave me was that I ate all that stuff without bread and show her the emptied vessel. One step-brother, in particular, was a hard ruffian. Once in a minor accident, he fell on the ground, a *rickshawala* took him to the hospital, informed home. When this chap recovered fully, he became cruel to all *rickshawalas* – would sit on any one, roam about all day long and when rickshawala asked for the payment, would abuse and sometimes beat him too. He always had money his mother gave. Among all of them, I alone was good at studies, always came first. In tenth, I topped the school. I had told you that I wanted to take the gold medal, which was given to the topper, I beseeched my mother repeatedly but she scolded me, forced me to write to the school that I would take cash in place of the medal. She said of what use is the medal, would rot in a corner, cash is of some use. Had it been the medal, it would have my name inscribed on it, life-long remembrance, which I could show to my children, who would have felt inspired.

My real brother was elder to me. He used to coach me at home. He would always say – 'you shall be what our father was, which none of his progeny, except you can become. I shall make you a doctor. One day when I was in the kitchen, my step-brothers came with the news that my real brother has put himself in flames in course of Mandal student movement. Breath stuck inside, I ran out to see him but they, my step-brothers, caught hold of me. They said – 'Police took him out of the fire, have taken away the corpse. No one from the family went to see him, nor did they let me go. No final rites were performed for him. My step-mother said – he was burnt all right, final rites got completed in his death itself.'

Even today before my eyes repeatedly flashes an image – fire blazing in the square, my brother burnt at his back is trying to come out of the fire, but each time he succeeds, is forced back into the fire by the crowd hanging around, my step-brothers at the forefront.

My brother was burnt alive, because he had none other than me. Had father been alive, probably this would not have happened. I cannot believe that he could commit self-immolation. He couldn't simply die leaving me behind. He was forcibly pushed into the fire, was redundant like me.

After brother's death, I was left all alone... but his dream accompanied me. To fulfill it, I had opted for the science-group, wanted to appear in the pre-medical competition but my husband didn't let me –"

She burst into tears. Prem Prakash tried to hand over his hankie; she pushed his hand aside.

"Please don't ever remind me of those days. What a torture it is to go through... you can't imagine."

Wiping tears with her dupatta, she turned her face to the other side. She appeared to be slightly angry with Prem Prakash, who himself was remorseful – what was the issue to start with and where did they end. She had come to him with a grievance. Trying to allay it, Prem Prakash became instrumental in causing intense pain to her. Her face was almost swollen – no image of real mother, early demise of father, such a death of the real brother, away from in-laws' house not one place where she could go, even for a few days, just to put herself in some different atmosphere. 'Mayka'... where?

"I feel I am a nomad wandering, God knows since when, in search of a home..." after a while she said –

"I didn't get my mother's home. The one I am currently living, I have been pushed into it. I dream of a home where I arrange everything with my heart, reside with the man I love, who is my husband, from whom I have children..."

Prem Prakash was shockingly surprised – she could dream! Those dreams further intensified her grief. The girl doesn't know about her mother, who might as well have been a nomad female. That's how this burning desire for a home in her progeny. Only female nomads are said to be so mad after love and home. Only they have this kind of zest for truth. Her father might really have fallen in love with a female nomad, who might have asked him to give her children and home; children he gave, home he could not.

"If you didn't get home of your choice, you may now have one. Who stops you? You can seek divorce, Prem Prakash got a little tough."

"Can you take divorce?"

Prem Prakash was shocked. To suppress it, he kept himself on the course –

"I mean, divorce is not something improbable in your generation. You are still young, beautiful. Anyone would be ready to take your hand. You can also get someone who accepts your son too."

"Of course, I can get... but I also seek something in him."

"What is it?"

"His heart should be gold, such as yours."

Prem Prakash's face was afire. Had he right then laid his fingers on it, would have definitely got the burns.

No one spoke for a while, waiting as it were for the fire on Prem Prakash's face to subside.

"I was a machine before I met you, lying in a corner. You touched, I became alive. No one touched me with such tenderness, advised like this. For the first time, I started feeling about myself – that I am also something and something can happen to me too, should happen. I was dead, became alive. Now I want to live."

"Who stops you? If for that you need to leave this home, build another... there is time for that too."

"And you don't have?"

"My life is almost over."

"How can you say that? Even if one is left with for twenty years only, a third of life is still left. And you, you would live for thirty years more at the minimum.

She was soaked inside, but her eyes bore a glow; threads of light pulled Prem Prakash towards them. Particles of fire lay almost extinguished inside both of them; she, pumping from her mouth, was slowly kindling.

Frankly speaking, you also seek her company. When you touch her, hold her in embrace, your heart and body get unified. You get the feeling of completeness... but you are content living that completeness in moments, whereas she wants to build home on it. She doesn't want to live in compartments, with time divided as of now – so much with you, so much in that home. You want the facility of coming back to the circle you live in, and leave only for a while.

Her feelings would be called love, whereas for you, it is tasting the sweetness of a relationship forbidden.

You call it compassion which might eventually be deepening into love.

You are bound, so is she, but she has the courage to make herself unbound. You lack it. You are a coward, a book-worm, she a butterfly, struggling to move out in the open.

"You are getting too far. Your gait has changed since you got a job. Now you don't even remember as to who got you qualified for it. When you came to our house, you were just intermediate. It was I who enabled you to complete further studies." Her husband complained one day.

"I put in the labour. Anyone may help but if the student doesn't study, nothing comes out of it" – she countered.

"Now you don't conduct yourself as you did earlier."

"How?"

"As a wife"

"How?"

"Do you take care of your husband?"

"Save two things, tell me what do I not do?"

"One may grant your not coming to the temple. I also won't like it, if you don't have faith, but have you seen any couple, who don't have physical relationship?"

"Whether there are such or not – I don't know; but I told you – I don't feel like..."

"You will do only your liking?"

"Yes."

"Your mind has been spoiled by your job and your conduct by contact with Prem Prakash. Every other day I have to hear the murmur that you move in his car, have amorous amusements with him."

"Dirty people have dirty minds."

"You mean I am dirty?"

"I didn't say it, you thought so."

"Stop meeting him."

"Why?"

"I don't like it."

"Only on this account? No place for my likes or dislikes. Who are you to decide about my likes or dislikes."

"Me...? I am your husband."

"I am your wife... but do I decide about your likes or dislikes?"

"It is husband's privilege... which prevails; you may check any household."

"I don't agree."

"Your agreeing, disagreeing has become so important that you don't care about others. We get a bad name that you move about with Prem Prakash... and you don't care? You sit with him in restaurants, in the dark corners of parks, move in his car. People taunt me, say that husband of this lady is an eunuch."

"And you put up with it? Who says so – let him face me?"

"You will have to stop moving with Prem Prakash."

"I can't."

"Why? What do you get from him. Save the job, what has that oldie given you – that which you didn't get from me?"

"It's not the age. Some contacts give you life, others kill you."

"You have started talking big – since you got employed. Earlier, this tongue didn't babble so much. You give up the job."

"And sit idle at home, as you do? How will the house run – have you ever given it a thought?"

"Do you think it runs with your salary right now?"

"No, but I do earn as much as my capacity. I at least bring to the extent of expenditure over me.

"Leave the job."

"I won't. I don't want to live like a dependent. You want me to leave it so that you kick me around."

"You learn all this trash from Prem Prakash, with whom you are whenever. What is he to you... aye?"

"He... he is 'everything'."

Words – cold and tough, uttered in passion which was her generation. God knows what insistence for truth, what craze... and heavens fell upon.

"Shut up... you bitch! Husband alive and she is out to woo another..."

"Husband is husband, not 'everything'" – she kept her cool.

" Then what is he?"

"He is husband, what else. A lump of rights, rights all the way, every step – with the feeling that he alone has the rights. What is a wife for him – cook food, wash clothes, share the bed whenever his lordship so desires, do this don't do this... and wife should always go on doing his bidding – yes sir, all right sir! She should go on giving you the satisfaction that your dictates are being followed. Husband – the eternal emperor, wife the slave perpetual."

"No use talking to this blighter..." muttering, the young guru left. The matter didn't end there. He thought of teaching her a lesson differently, planned while sitting in the temple-chamber, which was his office. He had already got main of the residential phone shifted here, extension being at the residence, so that he could overhear talks between her and Prem Prakash. Now he got a mobile for himself which was connected with the landline. When he was out, any call on the landline would get connected to the mobile as well. He always kept the mobile with him, so that when they talk in his absence – that also he could overhear. By now he was certain that her job is the spoiler; the day a woman goes out on a job, she sets flying. It is the job which has run her amuck – so first she should be got out of the job. Once confined to home, she will be a cow tied to the stand. She won't leave the job on his bidding, so it has to be planned – which he, sitting on his gaddi, did.

The director of the institute, where she was serving, started receiving anonymous complaints against her – some in writing, many more on phone – she is pervert, a keep of Prem Prakash, who has got her employed there. Anytime they can be sighted romancing in a park or a restaurant. Two houses on ruin..., etc., etc. To impress upon her that some outsider is sending the complaints he would tell her off and on – 'God knows who phones, abuses me – 'Bloody, impotent fellow! Your wife is being enjoyed by someone else, and you worshipping. The bird is set to fly away... get alert.' Whatever written complaints were being sent to her office, a copy or two thereof he got mailed to his address too. She was disturbed but kept her cool. Whenever the young guru told about the phones, she rebuked him – 'why don't you tell the caller to shut up; ask the fellow to face me, I will break his jaw.' In between, the young guru would counsel her – why don't you leave the job, what's four thousand bucks that our name gets maligned like this in the society. When all this had no effect, the young guru made one of his confidants to phone her – 'Blighter! You go out under the pretext of job, to enjoy with an oldie; have become his keep. If your husband is impotent, why don't you come to me, I will...' which was followed by lot dirty utterances. A threat at the end – 'all your amorous activities would one day appear in the newspaper, your photo with that oldie too.'

Right then, she scolded the caller but was perturbed nevertheless. Wasn't worried about bad name for herself... what was her name anyway! but Prem Prakash had a reputation which could be soiled. She would rather give up her job than risk his reputation. Disturbed, she rushed to him.

"This is no reason to leave your job" – he counselled. "Newspapers don't publish anything just like that, without any basis... are accountable. If they do it, they can be sued. It is not a news-material at all."

"Gossips related to a famous person like you can become news."

"Maybe, but they will act responsibly."

"And my employer?"

"That tribe doesn't have time for such trash. In this case, they know me pretty well. They also know that such things are common against a female employee, who is also beautiful and social. They are a professional lot, would just throw away such complaints in the dustbin. They are concerned with work – who is performing and with what efficiency and diligence – how useful a person is for their organisation. As a worker, you have a good name."

"But why should I not leave the job? What is four thousand bucks anyway? Honestly for me the job is only a pretext to get out of the house, where otherwise I would lie idle all day? Since he left the job, except for morning-evening rituals at the temple, he is always at home... would go on uttering whatever, try to clasp, touch me when I pass by. His touch... Oof! as if a lizard crept over... so nauseating! It is terrifying to imagine that I alone figure in his thoughts. He doesn't go out while I am in, tries to closet me as much as I try to avoid him. Sunday for me is difficult to pass."

"At night?"

"I make my son sleep between us. Even so, pretending to be in sleep, he would put his foot on mine. I never have a carefree sleep, am all the time anxious about his movements."

"Don't you feel it is being unfair to him? After all, he is your husband."

"The male in you speaking now. His very touch is nauseating, was so even before I met you. After you touched me, I feel my body to be sacred. If someone else touches, I feel as if mud has been thrown over me."

Prem Prakash didn't pay much heed, knew her to be a sentimental type... such thoughts would simply blow away in due course. Presently, he was occupied with the issue before them.

"Complaints to the institute, telephoning home... only someone who is deeply hurt over our relationship can go to this extent. Is there someone else who loves you?"

"Shit!"

"This leaves only two – your husband or my wife. My wife isn't that clever."

"Why, some of her friends, any relative, her brother might be backing."

"Maybe... someone whom she might have approached... but I doubt your husband more."

She suddenly fell silent; it had never occurred to her. Would he do such a thing which soils his own image as a husband? Could do it, for he is crafty alright. These days he is without any work – an idle mind a devil's workshop!

He might have thought that on his asking alone, she is not going to leave the job. Let it then be this way. He, who cannot imagine that without jobs we will be wholly dependent on father's pension, pushes his wife towards Harbhajan, could do anything!

She kept silent, knew that Prem Prakash's understanding of people is mostly correct.

"You are very much attached to your child, who needs both the parents. Quarrels between you two would be affecting him adversely. You should, therefore, adjust with your husband, everyone does. That way the hurdles which he is putting in your career... these complaints, telephoning, etc. would disappear."

"You neither understand me, nor yourself and certainly not what is between you and me. You go, adjust in your home, I don't need any such advice. First you put life in a corpse, when it gets moving... you push it back where it lay dead."

"I had in mind the future of your child."

"First, I have to keep alive. If I didn't, what child, whose child! I have gone through so much pain in my life that even a little happiness that comes my way, I want to hold on to it... dream of making it permanent. You want to take yourself away. If you had to do this, why at all did you draw me to yourself?"

Her face, which moments earlier was smooth, became swollen as if a sea-wave had just passed over the sand.

Whenever any of her favorite things was threatened to be snatched away, the anger, suppressed inside over the years, started shaking her entire body – as stormy winds shake an empty, weak building. She tried hard to hold, not let it out. Gathering her full strength, she tried to control her tongue, push inside the anger, which like volcano threatened to erupt any moment... for if it burst, it would simply burn out whatever came its way including those whom she loved, e.g. her child, Prem Prakash. Forced back thus for years together, the anger, piled layer upon layer, now lay inside her like a brick of fire, which could crack anytime and turn into a raging fire, out to swallow everything.

She lived on two extremes. One was this. The other... softness, which should have evaporated from her being by now... but was there... love which like thin rainy clouds, moved in her eyes, anxious to shower over Prem Prakash. At that time, her beautiful hands became all the more beautiful, her touch very cool, oozing out love. Prem

Prakash would put his mouth on her palm... what peace...! He wondered how such peace emanated from a person, so disturbed inside. It was not clear whether it was her love or thirst for love, which she never got.

But at this point of time, her eyes were hollow. Far below into them was dampness... which lingers in the eyes even after one has cried a lot.

The blankness which was on her face then sketched the image of a person who knew that she was loaded with a miserable past, which she has to carry to a future... that didn't exist.

"Decisions in life are not taken sentimentally. This kind of emotionalism only leads to self-torture. Facing every situation, analysing it objectively and then taking suitable steps – that is what is required."

"How can I help it, if I am like that."

It was largely true, she was made that way—impulsive, very emotional, getting charged up quickly and quite frequently. Outwardly proud and stubborn. Even in happy moments with Prem Prakash, she would suddenly get offended by some trifle; any off-hand remark or piece of a dialogue, would turn her into another being. Eyes burning, face swollen, she would hardly speak, only stare far ahead with hollow eyes – totally blank, as if her entire body had been squeezed. Her voice would suddenly change—coming, as it were, from some hole, deep inside; a voice soaked and heavy, as if it was of someone else. Such a change could occur any time, even in happy moments. Looked like she was cursed that happiness shall not stay with her for long, and she would be thrown back to her normal morbid state. As she had been in distress all along, may be, even a little happiness pinched her and instantly she pushed herself back to morbidity. On such occasions, Prem Prakash sometimes felt as if a ghost entered her being, dragged her out of the happy state and threw her back into morbidity. She would herself kick and scatter away things which built up those few happy moments. She wanted to hold on to them, but the moment they were threatened to get out of her hold, she slipped into the angry trance. Then no one could pull her out; it took weeks. All this while, her face would remain swollen, eyes stony, voice hoarse and damp. Prem Prakash imagined of the ghost because what put her off was very often such a trifle. For instance if she felt that Prem Prakash was not hundred percent with her at a given time she got off; some general remark Prem Prakash only casually made – she would pull it to herself and interpret it in a way that could cause her pain. Prem Prakash sometimes thought it was masochism, pure and simple... picking up pins and piercing them into yourself.

Instantly, she could not be counselled and brought out of her trance, was beyond reasoning then. Only way to bring her back to normal was slow and soft touches of love. Prem Prakash felt that each tissue of her being craved for love but he was also worried as to when would she learn to live naturally, how long would she continue to swing from this extreme to the other – one lost in love, the other fighting the ghost.

The ghost... was it of the first daughter-in-law of that house?

That day, however, Prem Prakash took her out of the town, in solitude, loved her. She, her face in Prem Prakash's neck, cried and cried.

She was in my lap. Tears rolling down. Quivering lips, smooth arms... I went on kissing. Her thick hair, beautiful face, dark eyes... flowers bloomed sometimes here, sometimes there! I rushed to pluck them with my lips, took them inside... fragrance lingering at plucking points. Transformed into a bunch of fragrance, she cried intermittently. A leaf, thousands of raindrops on

it... twisted with gushes of wind, drops of love sprinkled over me.

How strange! When in love, human body transforms itself like this... each moment.

Even when she was gone, fragrance lingered behind. When she would take me fully God knows what would she make of me! I want to go through that experience before leaving this world—when two beings blend to become one... their unfathomable love descending on their bodies.

The mere thought... lightening flashes inside.

Young guru had been keeping track of her all along, wanted now to catch her red-handed. Next time he followed her closely. He noted that she parked her scooty in the scooty-stand and got into Prem Prakash's car, waiting nearby. The car sped away. When she was home in the evening, young guru questioned her before his parents – "You have to tell today where have you been. You leave home for the office, go some place from there. His car waits for you, both of you go to some joint. Have to tell – where do you go? What's all this. Don't you feel ashamed?"

"Ashamed for what... for sitting in the car... of a person known to me, known to this house? I never concealed that I meet him. Shame for what? You should feel ashamed that you follow me surreptitiously..."

"I do because you are my wife. Come out now—where do you go, both of you?"

"Can't I go where I desire?"

"You have to tell me."

"Why?"

"I am your husband."

"Husband or master? Me a property and you priding over ownership of it... that too without fulfilling a single responsibility of a husband!"

She counter-attacked, which she did when pushed to the wall.

"Which responsibility! Tell me... What need of yours is not fulfilled?"

"Do you feel the responsibility for me and your child?"

"I do... I collect him from the school bus, on his return. Morning I am praying, so papa leaves him to the bus-stop. Do you ever go?"

"Had you been responsible, you would not have left the job."

"It is none of your business what do I do to earn. May not be from a job, I shall bring money from whatever source. How are you concerned. I shall bear all your expenditure and son's. O.K. Tell me what do you need? I have been crying hoarse that you bloody leave this trifle job. What is there... four thousand bucks!"

"A job is not simply to earn. Through it we perform our duty, improve our lot. We remain disciplined, save ourselves from being an empty mind, a devil's workshop. It doesn't lie with me as to what pay I am given as per my qualifications and current practices... but whatever... at least it takes care of my expenditure and boy's school fees."

"I will bear. You leave the job!"

"Expenses are not only the current ones. One has to think of boy's future too. Day after he will be due for admission to engineering or medicine; where will the money come from?"

"For everything, you get loan these days. When the need arises, I shall pick up the loan. None of your concerns."

"Sit idle at home depending upon loans, instead of being bread-earner for today and saving money for the future. That's your definition of husband's responsibility."

"And what obligation of a wife do you fulfill... tell me." – young guru said loudly, that the parents could also hear – "for years this blighter has not given herself to me. We do not have physical relationship... how are we husband and wife?"

He paraded me naked in the open market! The husband did it – one who is supposed to take care of his wife's prestige, provide her security. The matter related to two of us, a curtain hid it so far, he pulled it off. An issue which had to be settled only between two of us, he threw it open for public debate.

She felt her face burning.

"Very bad. Not a married woman's conduct," commented the father in-law.

Conduct expected of a wife – that she allows the husband – whatever he is and whenever he so desires – to mount over her, let him bite her flesh like a dog...? Lot more was boiling inside, struggling to come out in a vomit. It would have come out right then, had she not agitatingly headed towards her room upstairs. Young guru ran after, caught her by the arm, his other hand gripping her hair... pulled her back into the hall...

"You always run away like this, side-tracking the issue. It must be decided today, right now. Is it proper that wife is at home and I remain sexually starved? Your hunger gets quenched with that oldie, what about me – I, who happen to be young!"

"Stop it... this ugly stuff!" She shrieked. The fellow was bulging out all this before his parents and called himself religious?

"No, it must be settled today. I say before all these elders. You read this and sign..."

It was a stamp paper, as the one on which the sale deed for the house had been drawn. She evinced no interest in the paper put before her, so the young guru took it back and started reading loudly –

One: I will stop meeting Prem Prakash forthwith.

Two: Will go direct to the office and return home straight like a woman of character.

Three: If I have to go to a place other than the office I will dutifully inform as to where I am going and when shall I return.

Four: I will cook in the evening, presently done by Papa, will continue doing in the morning as of now.

Five: Will obey the husband and establish physical relationship with him with immediate effect.

'With immediate effect', as in official orders! Freedom to do the job had been granted – as money coming in was not such a bad idea to the three idle guys at home... but to go to the office and come back straight... like a machine! Can't have any desire, no right to wish... because she is a wife. Till now, she was exempt from cooking in the evening in consideration of her job. Papa cooked, for he liked it, a time-pass for him: Now that errand also passed over to her... punishment for her waywardness!

Young guru, after finishing, roared – 'sign it'

"Drama... all this..." She muttered.

"You call it a drama. I had it prepared by a lawyer."

God! The blighter narrated the story to the lawyer, made her naked there too!

Might have gone to Harbhajan, he had pushed her to for the tobacco dose! Who else... he knows only Harbhajan.

"I don't believe in all this. If papa has problem with night cooking, I shall do it. It doesn't require all this paper-work."

"So, you will continue to do your liking?"

"Yes, because I know I am not doing anything unworthy."

"Not even meeting Prem Prakash? Aye, what is cooking between you two?"

"One who talks in this dirty language simply can't comprehend the relation I have with him. This much I understand that whatever is between two of us – there is nothing unworthy about it."

"And that which you are doing with me – it's also not wrong?"

"No." She said coldly.

"Get out..." Young guru shouted. "Get out of our house. This is our house. If you don't care about the dignity of the house, you have no place here. Leave within a week..."

As if a tenant was being asked to vacate.

She went upstairs. Young guru kept shouting from down below. She bolted her room from inside, was now with herself, cries burst out. She could report to the police, complain to some institution dealing with domestic violence, but first they would prey with their searching eyes and queries. Then to keep up the show, the husband would be summoned. The moment, husband mentions Prem Prakash, he will have their full sympathy; they will agree with whatever he says. The husband will be provoked to give more and more detailed accounts to entertain them. Ultimately both sides shall be counselled – these are domestic matters, should remain within the confines of the house; the burden of maintaining prestige of the house is on her, she must obey her husband (the female police would say it more forcefully). And she will be sent back to get the same treatment from her husband after a while.

Funny! Years after marriage, son going to be eight and one fine morning you are told – 'nothing here is yours, get out...' just because you don't conduct yourself as he – the husband – desires! Even if things settle down today, sword of Democles would always hang over you. You can be shown the door even after twenty-five years of marriage. Only two words – 'get out!' Husband's house – parents send their daughter here and wash off! She kept sweeping, cleaning it, day in and day out as her house... and now told – she never belonged. Then what was she of this house – a maid or sweeper who is employed today and fired tomorrow? How to explain as to what is Prem Prakash Sir in her life? He put life into her, she started living only after meeting him. Even if she explains somehow, can these people rise to that level and comprehend? For them, earlier she was alive alright – was eating, sleeping, going to the college, doing all the domestic chores and also procreating! Dead you are now – they would say – when not conducting yourself as a housewife. Fear had seized her – 'Get out, leave within a week'. Order. Prem Prakash or no Prem Prakash. The decree can be pronounced anytime on any ground. Where does she stand in all this? Is there any thing here she could call hers?

Doing a job while living in this house – where neither salary, nor the house is yours? No security for future either. Salary – hand it over to the house, from where she can be thrown out any day... when she won't have a penny with her!

Constantly on the boil, she sometimes contemplates leaving this city itself. What about her son then? Overlooking it, if she still decides to go, the question remains – where to? Doesn't have any parent. Anyone in the city she came from? Uncle is there – father's younger brother, who in father's absence, had performed the rites of her marriage, Kanya-daan! Should she ask him? She with her son starts living separately in this town itself... can she with her meagre salary? That apart, whenever in a fit of rage she has hinted it, her husband had boomed back – 'the blighter doesn't have any prestige, I however have. People worship me here. My prestige will get maligned. Whisperings are already there; it will be the talk of the town; who will then come to my temple, take my blessings? She wants to uproot me from here?'

Prem Prakash was downcast when she told him.

"You stop seeing me. That's all he desires. What difference does it make."

"The issue is not of seeing or not seeing XYZ; it is about insulting me, about his rights and my freedom. Today, it is you, tomorrow he will say the same about another person. Means I should move only with one he approves of; if someday he develops dislike for that fellow too, stop meeting him forthwith, howsoever important that person be in your life."

"I am not that important in your life."

"You don't know; I do."

"Guiding you at times, sharing your tensions, miseries sometime – this we can do meeting secretly and occasionally. Tell him – all right, you will not see me."

"Meeting you secretly... I shall not be able to do. Why should I hide something I don't consider wrong at all. Why make a false promise?"

Prem Prakash – learned, and an intellectual – didn't have that morality which this ordinary girl possessed – morality inborn. Might have been in Prem Prakash too sometime... was lost when he became learned and practical, when he chose to be a successful person.

There could be some way out – Prem Prakash was exploring.

"The problem with him may not really be relating to your meeting y or z, but his sexual hunger. Can you..."

'No...' She interjected emphatically.

"Earlier you did have physical relationship with him."

"You were not in my life then."

"We don't have it between us... this physical..."

"Absence of sex alone doesn't matter. You touch me, embrace, caress and even kiss. Your love enters my being. Wind passes through the bamboo pipe to become flute-music. The pipe should be clean. Very touch of that fellow makes me feel dirty. I feel I am turning into a prostitute."

"But earlier...? You have a son."

"I never for a moment felt any pleasure with him. Only withstood it. Earlier I didn't think all that which gets into my mind now."

"Would you have felt the same, had I not been in your life?"

"Probably yes... whenever I reached this point of disgust. Any physical relationship without the base of love is prostitution."

"All married women do not love their husbands, yet they have regular sex with them?"

"They prostitute... some entire life; in my case it had to be only for few years."

"In our scriptures it is provided that a wife on bed with her husband should conduct herself like his beloved."

"Like only, can't be real one... till love sprouts in her heart. Until then it is only acting, that which prostitutes do. Besides, such prescriptions have been provided by males only."

"Conduct for husbands is also laid down."

"Then do they conduct themselves accordingly? A married woman doesn't ordinarily go out to serve. She seeks protection within the confines of her home. Before getting into a relationship with an outsider, she goes through enormous inner conflicts."

"It is possible that I might not be loving you while you do."

"That's not true, you know it."

"I, surely, do not love you as you understand it. You believe in sacrificing everything for love, I do not. For me, love is not all in life. Lovers when they come to live together soon get fed up with each other. Then feelings of isolation, loneliness, despair creep in. Some can't stand all that. Tolstoy's Anna commits suicide."

"These stories! I am not a character of the book – Anna or someone. I am a girl in flesh and blood, of my times. But leave it, I have not come to ask for your hand, but to seek advice. He has asked me to leave his house within a week and I also want to leave."

"Such things are only angry outbursts, quite common between husband and wife!"

"This kind of plastering... patching up, it's not me. I want to leave that house within a week, as asked by him."

"You are proud by nature, even proud of your pride... but you don't see how powerless are you. What can you do right now – you don't have a place to go. Where can you go?"

"That's what I have come to ask you." Her lips quivered to the left drawing a line on the face that side. A taunt lay latent there as if she was saying – come now, tell me... what are you going to do about it?

"I can go to my uncle, who in father's absence had performed my marriage ceremonies?"

"First he will only question you – what happened and why; he will then talk to your husband, who will complain – she doesn't give herself as wives do, is carrying on with someone else. On this point alone your uncle will find all faults only with you. Your husband will become the aggrieved party. Then your uncle will advise – you should never leave your husband's house. Now that is your home, your refuge. Everything of yours is his, women live like that only... etc., etc. If you insisted, that you will soon find a job, are in need of shelter only for a few days and he also agreed... conflicts would arise in his house from the day you start living with them. You will yourself get fed up and like to move out..."

"After all that has happened, can I continue living with these people?"

"O.K., take a small house on rent and move out with your son."

"I don't want to live in this town."

"Whatever you desire can't be realised always."

"Yes... and why should it be... what is there in me, what do I have..."

Suddenly, two big tear-drops peeped from each of her eyes – lingering in the corners. Prem Prakash felt helpless... as he usually did when with her. Reprimanding, scolding her in such moments appeared to be insipid.

"Will it be against your self-esteem if you tell your husband that you refuse to leave the house. You can't be turned out without being divorced."

"But I myself don't want to live there."

"Listen... you tell them that you will certainly move out but will do so as per your desire and convenience, say when you get a job in another city. Tell them that you could move to another house in this town itself... but are not doing so in consideration of the prestige of the house... so he should also be patient for the time being. As soon as you get a job in another town... you would yourself not stay."

That, to Prem Prakash, appeared to be doing justice with her sense of self-respect, was also closer to truth. She didn't care so much about the prestige of the young guru as for the prestige of the house... where she lived as a house-wife. She didn't have to worry about the job, Prem Prakash would try for the same.

New job... of a school teacher. New house, rented. One room only, compared to the earlier three-roomed house. Occupant – she alone, instead of five earlier. All left behind, Prem Prakash too. Only telephonic conversation with him as also with the man called her husband.

Young guru believed that she won't be able to move out... a girl, who couldn't travel alone even on the train...

how would she live in a new city, all by herself? And job... is it lying on a platter? Even if she gets one, will the pay suffice? She living alone, will be scared too, won't be able to manage without him.

She thought that she might be stopped at the eleventh hour by her in-laws at least, caring for the safety of their daughter-in-law... but it was in their presence that the young guru had shouted – 'get out'. Stopping her now would, therefore, be against their grain. They always toe the line of their son. All three of them kept mum when she informed that she had got a job in another town and she was going to join on such and such date. She got reservation done on the train with the help of Prem Prakash; the school arranged for her temporary accommodation in a ladies hostel. Rest she would manage on reaching. Opening managed, onwards she could decide by herself. Hostel was indeed a mess, so she with the help of ads acquired on rent outer portion of a family's house. Prem Prakash had given her some money while coming. With that and her salary, she purchased essential things, including a mobile. Duly intimated her mobile number to the husband and in-laws. However, no phone from them... as if they were convinced that it was a matter of time that she would return defeated; and no third place for her to go. Prem Prakash telephoned her almost daily, patiently listened to all that she had to say and at the end mostly said – You know better, only you have to decide. He wanted to see her as a perfect working woman – rational, practical, decisive, self-dependent and confident. He would not get carried away by her sentiments which still had sway over her. She felt lonely and quite often cried on the phone. Prem Prakash consoled – 'very soon you will have lots of acquaintances there and will be in your elements.'

She suffered pangs to talk to her son, phoned frequently to get a chance. When she requested that he be called on phone, there were excuses – 'he is playing outside, no one here to call, we called, but he refused, he doesn't feel like talking to you?' Sometimes they put her on hold – 'just a minute, calling'. She held on at this end but no one came at the other: They were happy to let her bill swell this way. It was obvious that young guru had suitably briefed them – she has gone on her own (though it was he who had kicked her out), so let her suffer. Once per chance the phone was picked up by the son, who told her – no one ever informed him about the mother calling, he wanted so much to talk to her. She made him take down her mobile number, asked him to talk whenever, prefixing it with zero. The boy did call once or twice; there was silence again. Thereupon when once again per chance he picked up, she learnt that young guru had seen the boy dialing and had got the S.T.D. facility removed from the landline. He had mobile for his own use anyway.

Months passed and she was not able to have a word with her son. She was overtaken by depression. Loneliness she could fight keeping herself busy with school-work. Anxiety about her son, however, deepened – how, must he be, anyone giving him meals on time, going to school regularly? Must be getting scolded in the school for not doing home-work, constant reprimands would be making him shameless, developing distaste for studies.

The stream of such thoughts led her only to one conclusion – coming here, leaving her son behind was a mistake. Respect – is it such a big issue that son be left behind to perish? Why couldn't she imagine that there was none to look after him, once she left. Women bear all kinds of ordeals for the sake of their children. She is selfish.

Right then came the inner voice – she can look after the son but first she has to survive.

This man is such a butcher. Animosity is with her... but they are punishing the son. Not mother alone, it is natural craving in a son too; they should let him talk to his mother... for child's sake. If her husband is cruel, the seniors – her-in-laws, who have seen the world – should feel compassion for the boy? They appear to have decided to let him get used to living without his mother, as do children whose mother is no more; he will soon forget his mother, not even recognise her when she comes. Would she ever go back? She has not separated, has not come here immediately following any heated exchange, didn't remind them about the old rancour either. She had just informed that the new job was better than the present one, hence she was going. They didn't stop her even once. Had they, she might have reconsidered. Separation – this certainly is not, nor leaving the in-law's house for good.

Rita madame, head of her department. Experience in teaching plenty as fat on her body. Just can't avoid her. Hungry look, always eager to know – what this new girl is? Where does she live? Husband? She had to lie constantly – 'yes, husband resides with her, is in a touring job, reaches home late, sometimes not able to reach'.

'Nothing in the house?'

'Brought only what was essential. Not sure about permanency of the job here.'

'Dear me... there should be something at least for guests to sit?'

How to tell her – if the intention is not to let anyone in? Who will face such piercing queries. Happy alone. But Rita mam forthwith sent two cane chairs and a table – 'were surplus in her house, occupying space unnecessarily, there should be something to sit on, when she comes here.'

'You are my junior colleague dear. It is my responsibility to look after you. Why have you not brought your son along?'

'First, let me be permanent here mam! His school can't be changed frequently'.

'You two here, who looks after the child?'

'In-laws'.

'I see'.

Queries like arrows, one after another. Mam's love helter-skelter, like flesh on her body – "You would be missing your child. I shall leave my youngest daughter to be with you here everyday for an hour; pass time for you after school hours. You may check her school-work, etc., chitchat with her. I shall pay you Rupees five hundred a month, your salary being meager presently...".

School regulations prohibited tuitions. Senior teachers of the same school inventing a bye-pass! Mam didn't say as much, but her experienced eyes had seen that the husband of the girl was not on good salary, why else his wife should come this far for a job. In the school, what was her pay like, mam already knew. The girl is needy.

Now for an hour, sometimes two... she is coaching mam's daughter, rather putting up with her. Sometimes plays with her, tells her stories... The poor child is mentally challenged, is studying in this school thanks to mam, wouldn't have got admission elsewhere. Till their daughter is here, mam and her husband can roam about carefree. On her part she, politely declined the tuition-fee. Had she accepted, Rita madam would have a handle to pressurise her, whenever desired.

She appreciated the Principal. Good looking, smart, walks briskly... as if not only the school, life itself is in her firm grip; intelligent, rational, controlled in speech; nothing sluggish around her. Everything redundant is just thrown away, as trash which incidentally fell upon her sari. Teachers in the school simply pale in her presence.

Prem Prakash wants to see her in this model!

She is infatuated by Principal madam's personality but doesn't like her ways: one can see the madam toe-toing school owner's representative, who comes frequently, sits in a big room next to Principal's. In a school, no one above the Principal should have an office... but those who have invested in the school want both – profit and power, school will run any way. So the Principal who moves amidst her colleagues like a tigress, turns into a fox before a chap, who is almost illiterate. When the owner happens to come, the Principal mam spreads red carpet from the main gate to school's entrance, lady teachers lining on both sides with a rose in their hands. Taking flowers from them each, the fellow with a paunch, stamp of foolishness on the face makes his grand entry into the school. A fellow, who knows only how to invest and make money, passes through the ladies as Prince Saleem through Anaarkalis!

And all this is arranged by Principal madame; wish she could speak up – 'a female teacher is teacher, not a slave-girl.' In our society even the first female who would have stepped out for earning, would not have gone through such an experience.

Principal mam scolds any teacher before anyone, even before the students – 'this blighter would see me out of the job...' 'now either you would remain here or me...' such language doesn't behove her, filmy language as that of the illiterate owner. Luckily, she doesn't use such language before parents, to whom she is so polite, so accommodating. In the school, you can't scold a child, whatever his/her fault but on parents day Principal mam can scold any teacher even before the parents and the student. They are precious to the owner, hence to the Principal too because they bring money/donation. Through them, more people will come, more money. So, whatever the parents say about their children is acceptable. On parents' day, the school turns into a courtyard of rich fellows, where whatever their pet says has to be obeyed. Other days, it is a shop.

Principal Mam is head of the school. She should think big – things like purpose of real education, targets set by the school in this behalf, future of children, etc.; should inspire her subordinates but she is all the time busy about pleasing the owners of the school, projecting herself before them. She doesn't ever appear to think as to what the Principal of a school should really be, how is she viewed by children and their parents, by the teachers and the citizens of the town.

Hard task-master to new-comers like her, she always keeps them on toe and under tension, scolds them left and right. Says she is inculcating discipline into them, educating them but the new-comers need encouragement too. They should not just get fed up at the very beginning of their careers. As it is, there is hardly any career anywhere these days. She will be squeezed so long here. They want new teachers to get fed up soon and leave – regular movement, less expenditure on replacement! There is also power in recruiting. Besides, the new recruits are a subdued lot, while the experienced ones throw their weights around. Permanent faculty may be a good idea for the school and the children but they just don't care. She knows what her career is going to be – leave one school and join another, that shop after this one!

Like Rita Mam, other female teachers are also curious to know why has she come this far to serve, why serving at all and not living at home. They try to explore it in multiple ways despite being academically convinced about female upliftment and the fact that a woman can be independent only when she is so economically. This is the first step... but they relish seeing other females enslaved at home.

She doesn't encourage anyone to visit her, tells everyone that her husband is home in the evening... but two managed anyway – Rita Mam and Rahul Sir. Mam is head, feels it is her right. As for Rahul Sir, she had to take his help while fixing up this apartment on rent. For certain tasks males are needed at the front line. Else landlords feel free to put all sorts of silly questions to a single girl – where do you come from, who are there at home, who is here, husband works in which company, his designation, salary... they will go on. If a male accompanies you, he would put a full stop in one reply – she is working in such and such school, its reputation you know, you will get your rent regularly and on time. Finished. She may be obliged to Rahul Sir but he can't visit her as a matter of course, as can Rita Mam, being a female. He is however making efforts by trying to invoke pity – "recent marriage but marital life disturbed – wife very ambitious, not happy at all with his degraded profession, calls it third rate, doesn't stay here, comes only sometimes, marriage won't last, he lives alone, self-cooking...."

She never enquired about Rahul Sir or any other colleague for that matter. Everyone has something or the other to hide, should have the freedom to do so.

Rahul Sir is a risky preposition, every man is. Little lift and... so she has to be tough, tight all the time – a strain all right, but she just can't afford to sit and relax with a male. A woman living alone... any window left little open and anything can happen. She took care to meet Rahul Sir only in restaurants but once he sneaked in – "wants to meet her husband, can wait...." She wriggled out – "have to go to Rita Mam's right now." Attraction for a girl living alone lurks in Rahul Sir's eyes.

Why blame others, she is also changing. Every third lady, she saw in town was in pant-shirt, sitting on the scooter with a male companion; she bought jeans and shirt for herself. The attire was prohibited back home. Earlier in step-mother's house she was first a child, became a labour when grew up. Urge to wear pant-shirt lay suppressed in her all the while. She felt the air of independence when for the first time she sat in Rahul Sir's scooter in pant-shirt, shoulder to shoulder with men, flying. Thought of buying one more set... else Rahul Sir would think she has only one which she wears repeatedly.

She sits behind Rahul Sir on his scooter, by his side in the restaurant, but never felt like touching him – a desire which springs instinctively for Prem Prakash. Can she ever talk with Rahul Sir in that vein. This man doesn't have depth, is frivolous. Getting some odds done here and there with him and in exchange sitting with him over a cup of tea occasionally as you do with a colleague – that's enough. Whenever Rahul Sir tries to make advances she politely reminds him that they work in the same school where intimacy between colleague is not taken nicely. It won't be good for either of them, so better take care.

She, who sometimes even boasted of being always on the side of truth, now shields herself behind lies. Tells lies one after another about her husband. There are so many ladies nowadays, who didn't pull on with their husbands and started living separately. Prem Prakash had given the address of a divorcee lady here living alone. Her colleagues and friends visit her whenever they like. This lady is so natural in or out of her premises. No complex, no worry as to what one thinks about her. She called on her, enough to tell that she works in a school, has come through Prem Prakash. She was so affectionate. 'Anything required any time, tell unhesitatingly' – she assured her. She, however, didn't visit her again.

Their circumstances are different. The lady doesn't have a kid, is lecturer in the university. People have broader outlook over there. In the school, one has to show off... to children, to their parents. There is much emphasis on character here... because they have to lure. Matter of a lac or two per admission. Public school after all. Both manager and Principal are never tired of repeating that their teachers have to be role models, have to have character. Teachers with broken marriages or heading towards one are bad examples. 'We don't employ them' –

they openly say. However every one knows about Rahul Sir and the English teacher Pramila. They are exceptions, having come through source. Pramila openly says – "yes she and her husband are incompatible... so what. This is our personal matter." Compared to Pramila, she being from small town is timid, has kept her private matter carefully suppressed. Deliberately repeats that she would get her son admitted in this school only, after becoming permanent. The lie about her husband gets buried under the truth about the child. She was also contemplating about taking a full-hedged flat next year, putting a double-bed in the bed-room there, so that people get convinced that her husband does reside here. People normally don't examine the bed-room closely... but flat? Can she afford with her small salary? Will have to take help of Prem Prakash, who always assures her – "don't worry about money, don't put yourself to any difficulty on this score." But to take his help for essential things is alright, flat is a different proposition. He would call it – luxury.

She is out of her home for the first time. Stranger in the new city, her loneliness and being away from home... that's why probably she talks a lot on phone... always serious, feelings oozing out... I am carried away. Feel lot of love for her, am further convinced that age is no bar to feel love.

She says – 'you are always thinking; this tribe reaches nowhere, should stop pondering'. She may be right. We continue to think and some rare exhilarative experiences which life had in it's bag and was out there to pour into our lap... they go by.

Thinking takes us away from reality, weakens our resolve to change it, makes us cowards almost.

Initially there was passion in my love for her. But the more I came to know her, the more I began thinking about her, it turned deeper and deeper. Passion thinned out. She was more than a female body, was a person, a being.

I thought all the more about her, about myself, about us both. Can anyone stop thinking, I certainly cannot. If she is made that way, well... As far as I am concerned, I can't stop thinking, even if I wish to.

The difficulty is that real thinking not yet set in, life moved on in the meantime; it has taken a leap... and thinking is left limping behind.

My compassion reached her as love. No, in me too it might have been compassion in the very beginning, turned into love soon thereafter. To bridge the gap of age, however, I kept convincing myself that it was only compassion. Kept deluding myself as I do for so many other things. But love it surely was. Not possible without it to get so deep in the pain and distress of another person. She quickly recognised it and cutting aside wild creepers of age-difference etc., very soon reached the point where she could feel the delicate touch. With it came the desire to live. Source thereof or anything contributing it – how can ever be wrong or unworthy?

I thought – once the wounds of her feathers got cured, the little bird would be able to fly. I told her – "you are in a new city on your own, my wounded little bird is recovering fast, shall soon fly away into the sky. She retorted – the bird doesn't want to recover, is happy in her nest closeted with her wounds."

Much younger and less thoughtful, she is gifted with lot more courage than what I have. Adverse circumstances make me feel downcast, like an animal on seeing the barrier of the cage. Of course, I have lot to lose, she has nothing; I think of distant future too, she doesn't think of even two steps beyond.

She says – 'if our relationship hurts someone, why should we care. Did anyone ever stop to ponder how much pain is being inflicted on me. Unavoidably happiness comes only at the cost of causing pain to one or the other. If the other guy has a soul, I too have it. Why hurt me? To live for oneself is not being selfish, certainly not always. It's a way to happiness.' But do you really get happiness that way? Even if you do, it is temporary. If two of us were to live under the same roof, it is quite possible that soon we would get tired of each other, this love would surely not last. Later on, a doubt may also raise its head – the castle we built for ourselves on the foundation of pain to our family members... was it worth it? This situation has been portrayed in so many novels.

There is substance in her saying that she in flesh and blood belongs to the present, never lived earlier. She can't be transfixed in any book's frame. But if we don't keep those instances before us, how do we surmise as to what can happen to us. She says – "you can know about it only after it has happened, after we have lived it. Why should we presuppose that we would get tired of each other, as has been depicted in the books. It can also be that living together deepened love.' She says there is no up and down in love. True love appears only at the peak, remains there, ever opening novel angles with its light. It lifts us if we fall, filling us with life all the time. Its depth and intensity remains the same... expressions keep varying. Moon is always full and round, only appears reducing or increasing at times."

Ironically though not much adverse has happened in my life, yet I always feel that nothing here is permanent. Momentary flash, finished. On the other hand, she constantly lived amidst adverse and terrible and yet she can think that our relationship would always last.

A romantic dreamer! That's why she gets disappointments one after the other; I wish—she was little rational too.

Compared to other societies, the Indian society appears to me to be rather aggressive and cruel. Despite big talks, e.g. all beings are only part of the Super-being, there is no respect of humanbeings in our society. West, they hold that life on earth alone matters, nothing afterwards. Therefore, an individual in this life should have full freedom in matters of relationships, and the way one wants to live. Here we constantly put ourselves on the altar like sacrificial animals to shape the next birth, one is not sure of. There they have only the individual, here there is a big net over him – parents, siblings, children, grandchildren, God knows who else. The moment an individual takes a step of his or her choice, all these utensils start crackling. All your achievements in life can perish at just one honest belief of yours – that at this juncture you want to live with such and such.

Nisha's visits to young guru had increased since his wife's departure. Parents of young guru gave full liberty to them. Prompt replacement of their daughter-in-law... suited them. No matter that the arrangement was unofficial, concealed and temporary... Nisha was around for almost the whole day. They could while away their time with the T.V., while the new couple could be alone in the temple or upstairs. Their main concern was that their son should be happy because he was the only son left and his wife had left him unfulfilled.

Nisha and young guru met every second or third day, skipping morning-evening prayer-time. Sometimes, if the boy was away in the school Nisha would head straight to the house, telephone young guru, who would come over instantly from the temple. They would then have the desired solitude in the upper room occupied by Guru's real wife earlier. If the boy was in, they would sit in the inner portion of the temple. Sometimes Nisha authoritatively entered the kitchen, cooked whatever for herself and the young guru, served the parents too, exchanging pleasantries with them. She moved in the house like a de-facto housewife with their implied concurrence. They were happy as parents generally are on the arrival of the new bride. Very soon, however, anxiety sneaked in.

"My parents have again taken up the issue of my marriage..." Nisha told the young guru one day.

'Why? Three years are not yet over, stars continue to be unfavourable.'

"They had shown my horoscope to some shastri, who opinin that the stars were never unfavourable for marriage."

Young guru felt embarrassed, but didn't show.

"Perceptions differ sometimes, but who told you that they are making efforts again?"

"Yesterday they showed me some photographs and sought my choice."

"Liked any?" Young guru asked with a crooked smile.

"Come on..." pouring love, Nisha sheepishly looked at the young guru. "Our meetings shall get curtailed once 'Didi' returns."

"She is not going to come back."

"You do not love her at all?"

"That bitch! I told you – she allowed herself to be the keep of an oldie. Is throwing her weight around on his strength only. I turned her out. With what face would she return?"

"Do you love your son?"

"I don't know how he got conceived because behavior of that bitch was bad from the very beginning. She bred distaste. It must have happened in some moment of weakness. Now he is there as a fact of life, responsibility, which has to be borne. We have to live in the society."

"Do you really love me?"

"There is no one else in my life, you know. On the gaddi, I listen to the sorrows of others, but there is none to here mine, except you."

"Can you leave your wife and son for me?"

"She has already moved out, some day would take away the son too."

"Will you marry me?"

"Formality of marriage... is it really necessary? You know in our society, divorce is not viewed sympathetically. Why can't we live like this only. In the West they do... they call it 'live in relationship'. The son also gone, we shall have all freedom. As it is, the house is that side, my abode is here. Then, we can always go out of the town, spend a few days there in some good hotel. We can spend the night in this room too whenever you so wish."

"If I want to have children?"

"Population in our country is on the increase. So many unemployed... why further increase their number. First the slogan was – we two, our two; then it came down to one, now it is none whatsoever. Why spoil our lives with uncalled for responsibilities. We are fine this way, marriage is hardly necessary."

"Will my parents be ready for this kind of arrangement?"

"Tell them that you don't want to marry just now because of your studies, will think about it later. Thereafter hang on under the pretext of finding a compatible. Obviously they won't agree for me – married, father of a son... they would say. Even if I get divorce, they will find out other deficiencies, e.g. is a divorcee, unemployed, dependent on parents, etc. People in our country do not appreciate spiritual pursuit, which is our heritage; it calls for forsaking worldly actions. You keep procrastinating marriage. What is there which can't be between us now? So, let it drift. As soon as you cross a certain age the danger shall disappear automatically. If we continue like this only, our love shall also last long."

Nisha, for the first time, was disappointed with the young guru. He has proved his point alright with one argument on another... but there was something missing.

Even if they could live like this, it won't be spending life with one's life-partner. Of course, there must be something in this arrangement whereby it is so prevalent in the West. There within this framework they have also children who are accepted in the society. It has also started in our country lately.

Why think that far at this point of time. Let parents continue their search. Difficult to find really suitable and someone she also approves of. Will cross the bridge when it comes. Until then...

Time is being nicely spent. The young guru caters to her needs, her desires, looks after her parents, her house. Is always ready to do things, is such a support.

"Sometimes, I get late here. You have to drop me... then return. You said you shall buy a bike for me."

"Anytime."

"Whenever your savings permit?"

"Why wait till then. It was the way earlier. We live in different times – acquire now and enjoy... pay with loan, repay loan comfortably. Tomorrow itself we can go and pick up the bike. Why stretch our inconvenience."

Disappointment, which had descended upon Nisha a short while ago, disappeared. Young guru cares, tries to fulfill all her desires.

"Guruji! going not good without Guruain, people talking all sorts of things, reputation going down."

He was one of the favorite pupils of young guru – of his inner most circle, comprising of three-four loiters who with their chronic sycophancy kept him in a good humour. When his intimate ones have such ideas what buzz would be in the heads of general disciples falling in the outer circle? They may not say on his face. Young guru was upset.

"What do they say?"

"They say that your guru no longer has his heart in religious matters. Sometimes he doesn't come to the temple even for morning-evening 'aarti', sends his father instead. Roams about on the scooter with a girl, sitting behind him. She is the devil. Guruain left because of her. Incapable of putting his own house in order, your guru has the pertinence of advising others."

Outwardly, the young guru wore a smile, but the prick had penetrated, and it stayed there. Those who think that his wife went away because of Nisha, must be imagining much more. He and Nisha might be under surveillance. Who knows it is his inner circle spreading such shit out of jealousy.

Young guru was not feeling the winner even when he, along with his son, had gone to see off his wife at the railway station. He had persuaded himself to act altruistic. After all we do help people in situations like boarding the train – then, a woman, going out of the town for the first time! Son was also keen. However, once she was gone, young guru deliberately kept reserve so as to implant in son's mind that his mother was cruel, left her son behind for the sake of her ambitions and selfish motives. The young guru could have followed her to help her settle down at the new place, but decided to let her face it alone, so that she breaks down eventually. But today when Ratneshanand (title conferred by young guru) informed that his wife leaving him is not being taken nicely, the young guru felt the prick. If this is what people think and if the same process continued, his reputation shall be mired in no time and the titles of 'Swami', 'Anand', etc. decorating the board outside his house shall soon bite the dust. He has been playing wrong, should play it reverse. Wife settling down in another town spelt doom for his trade. Before the devotees he has to set up his own example of being an ideal house keeper, a good '*grihastha*'. Our country is like that only. People worshipping gods and goddesses seek clean image in their gurus. He will have to show off, can have freedom only behind the curtain. If people kept talking like this, word shall someday reach Swami Anoopanand maharaj – from whom the young guru had taken the 'deeksha' – and he might land here anyday and publicly disown him! He is quite capable of doing it.

Young guru's dirty mind set scheming. U turn, seat of the guru must be protected, only way to have both income and Nisha. Before his wife fully settles down there and refuses to return, something has to be done, else it will be too late. Cast the net wide.

And the coming days saw sudden change in his behavior towards his wife. Now not only did he permit his son to talk to his mother, connect himself if there was no phone from her over a period of time. Towards the end of their talk, he would himself get in and ask about her well-being. One day he proposed that he could come over to assist in properly setting up her house. Hearing it, shiver ran over her body.... With him alone! He could rape her. If she got something done through him, God knows what he would do or demand in exchange. Meeting the school people here, he might play some mischief. She declined point-blank, enough that he stays there, looks after the son – that he eats properly, goes to school regularly. She asked him to help the boy in the homework assigned by the school, get him a good tutor. She can send two thousand rupees per month for this. To the young guru refusing money was always an insult to Goddess laxmi – but he acted as if he was accepting it reluctantly – she may send only when the tutor is fixed, only that much which is his fee, should not send whenever in difficulty, he will somehow arrange at this end.

He manoeuvred through his son... cajoled him to tell his mother that he missed her very much. When Siddartha spoke sentimentally like that, she burst into tears, was depressed thereafter for hours.

She decided to go to her son during Diwali holidays – after all she has not come here as a sequel to any big feud, nor had she told that she is leaving for good. Her son being there, it won't occur to anyone that she has gone for ever. He said – 'get out'. She did get out but in a civilized way – that no outsider would even know about it. It would be in the fitness of things if she kept going there now and then, everyone would naturally conclude that she had gone only for the job.

When she reached, the young guru was present at the station with the son and a bouquet of flowers. Was running on the platform to and fro, looking for her in this compartment or the other. He was in pant-shirt to please her. Accepting the bouquet, she formally thanked him, as she did in the school... and ran to clasp her son.

The first thing she did on reaching home was to see Siddartha's school diary. Was shocked to see that in the previous tests he has failed in all subjects except Hindi. Reprimand of the class-teacher was on record, also the fact that his attendance in the school was poor.

"Why were you not regular in the school?"

She asked him before everyone, so as to question them too. Siddartha kept silent. It was young guru who replied –

"He was. However after you left, he didn't keep well. When he felt he was not well, I didn't force him to go to the school, his illness might have aggravated."

"This way you also arranged for your holiday – not sending, so no picking up either. Did he go for tuition?

"Discontinued only last month. Whenever I went along with him, the tutor madame was not present. I fired her, am looking for another."

"Did you meet her even once, or telephone her? Teachers normally are not irresponsible."

"She isn't that tribe. Those who do not have any job, take to tuitioning or coaching these days."

"You could have found out a better one."

"Am searching, will get soon."

The in-laws sitting on the fence were just watching. For them happiness of their son was supreme. Young guru happy, they were happy too. They were not bothered about the future generation because they knew they won't be there. They were not concerned whether Siddartha studied or not. They are going to leave behind this house which they have put under joint ownership of the young guru and his wife, so that young guru may not sell it out. The grandson is thus well taken care of. He will have a house in anycase; as for bread and butter, everyone is able to manage by hook or by crook. The father-in-law kept mum, mother-in-law however murmured – 'the boy is not going to be a 'laat-sahab' on getting educated.' When everyone had dispersed, she whispered to the young guru – 'if she is so serious about the boy's studies, why doesn't she take him along. Tell her that the boy doesn't listen to anyone except her.'

But the young guru was on his game – wife living there, earning... even if she sends money for son's education here, what does he gain if his disciples start suspecting him, scrutinizing his affairs. He would lose his clientele. She enjoying there, constraints on the young guru here; wife at home... there is prestige in the society. It also facilitates Nisha – her parents will not object, if she stays here longer, even late at night. As it is, wife doesn't go to the temple side; Guilty over Prem Prakash, she doesn't have the face to object to his affairs with Nisha. She will be wife for appearance's sake, Nisha the real one. Any man worth the salt has minimum two wives. Living here, she will take care of the domestic odds e.g. cooking, look after the son; he, carefree, can immerse himself in his affairs. Settled there, she goes out of his grip. She will taste the blood of freedom, will get accustomed to living alone. So he has to unsettle her there, compel to return. Not only now, whenever she tries in future to settle down anywhere outside... go and burn the 'Lanka!'

Outwardly detached, young guru kept acquiescing – 'Yes, as you decide, boy's future after all, you know better, etc., etc.' If she spoke tough, he put up a docile appearance.

Can she take Siddhartha with her? Service not permanent, remuneration not adequate, only one rented room by way of house! No one to share her responsibilities, will have to take the help of Rahul Sir or another man at every step. His expectations!

Even if she takes Siddhartha along, she won't put him in her school. Everyone there would dig out from him things she kept concealed so far – where is your father, why doesn't he stay here, his occupation! The boy's studies, already in shambles would go to pieces in a few months only. Will he get admission in any other school there? Even if admitted, he won't be able to pull on with the students there, will break down mentally, may become a psychic! Out to shape his future, she will end making the poor thing a mental case', may even loose him... she thought far ahead.

Sometimes, she feels – it is she who is at fault. She wants things only her way, not prepared to sacrifice anything. She wants freedom and also security of home, husband but not his tyranny, damns society but cares for what people think, tries to keep appearances.

She thought she could discuss with the husband, who appeared to have cooled down after the jolt her departure had given him.

"Studies of Siddhartha are in bad shape. Take care, else he may not clear the annual exam."

"What can I do if he listens only to you. On my part I give full attention."

"Next year, I shall take him along but I fear this year his performance might be so poor that not only does he not get promoted here, admission in any school becomes difficult there. Even if admitted, he will not be able to pull on. The students over there are very smart in studies, ten times more than what they are here."

"You do one thing, put him in a hostel."

"Whoop! What a great idea! Doubtful that he can cope normally, how would he as a boarder? He would get spoiled over and above; he is in a tender age, not suitable for a hostel and by the way have you any idea how much would it cost!"

"Don't worry – money will come. We put fifty-fifty."

The young guru always built castles in the air – she knew it. When she didn't react, the young guru played his card –

"You take up some job here only. Siddhartha then would be under your direct supervision."

"I was doing it, why did you then say 'get out'."

"Forget... forget it."

Whistling mildly, he was throwing the air out of his mouth, signalling that she should also similarly throw all that out of her mind. She detested this method of his cajoling.

"Is it that easy? I am not like you – now this, quite opposite next moment! I gave up a regular job here, searched one in another city, appeared in the written and viva voce for it, found out a house there, set up the household... did all this. Can you imagine how much pain I must have felt over what compelled it?"

"Happens... happens in anger."

"It wasn't just anger of a moment. You repeated throughout the week – "Get out". Who will live here after that? I can earn for my livelihood. As for the son, he is of us both. You have to share the responsibility."

"I don't deny. Told you – put him in a hostel. I will pay half... from wherever."

"Not his age for such a thing. You told me – how even a mild rebuke, he takes it to his heart, keeps moaning to himself in a corner, stops eating until someone cajoles. Such a boy can't be put in a hostel."

"Do one thing... you come back."

"Come back... and then again 'get out'. There is no guarantee that it won't happen again. You must have shouted thousand times that this house is yours and at your mercy I live here."

"Now I shall give it in writing, on a stamp-paper."

Stamp paper again... similar to the one which he had brought earlier, his conditions inscribed on – she shall do this, not this. She very much remembered it.

Job here... now, is it that easy to get? If you tell him, he would promptly respond – 'where is the necessity, he will bring money from wherever. But now job is a must for her, she will never be dependent on him economically.

She kept it at that. First she has to think it over by herself – what does she want!

Siddhartha may be very young but he can also have an opinion which she should seek. Quite possible that the boy has a soft corner for his father or who knows these people might have brainwashed him. He is a weakling, looks as if cramped, always fearful and despondent. So after the reprimand on her arrival, she now sat with him alone to lend a delicate touch.

"Siddhartha dear, why do you not go to the school daily?"

"I don't like it." He moaned.

"See all the boys go to school. If you won't study, people will laugh at you, call you 'illiterate' when you grow up. You will be incapable to earn, to marry."

"This school is no good. They scold all the time."

They do it because you are weak in studies. If you improve, go with your homework done, why would they?

O.K., next year we put you in another school. Complete this standard here, can't change in mid-session... you know. And why don't you eat properly."

"The same stuff is cooked everyday, doesn't taste."

She is moved to tears whenever she looks at him. Poor thing! Caught between two grinding stones – father and mother. Now a complete orphan. In her absence, who would be asking him as to what does he want to eat.

'You tell Dadi whatever you want to eat.'

Siddhartha didn't say a word. She continued looking at him, lost in himself.

"Does Papa beat you?"

"No. He doesn't even scold. He is nice."

"Does he bring whatever you need?"

The boy gestured affirmation.

"Do dada-dadi scold you?"

"No."

"See, my boy. I shall fix up your tutor, send money from there for the tuition. Now put your heart in studies. Once you are good there, you would come to like the school."

"Mama, why don't you stay with me?"

Oh my sweet one! What can I say... she was crying inside but put up a brave front.

"See my boy! My job is there. If I don't earn where will the money for your expenditure and mine come from?"

"You are a teacher. Can be one here too. There are so many schools here. Stay with me Mama, please, I feel bad without you..."

She clasped him... she too feels bad without him. His body's smell, presently filling her nostrils, emanates when he sleeps by her side. How much does she miss it! Sometimes she feels – all her feuds with the young guru, her hatred for husband and this house... all that stuff is dirty foam on the surface; under current is of clean water... her son, love for him. Let them insult her as much they like... even beat her, she should stay with her son.

She collected herself.

"You want to stay with me?"

He nodded.

"Then this year you study well here. Next year I shall take you there, get you admitted in my school but for that you have to score well in this class. Do you want to come with me?"

"Yes."

"You won't have papa there."

The boy didn't say anything; something was churning inside him. Only when mother was getting up, he uttered in a slow tone.

"Mama, can't it be that Papa also comes along."

Her jaws clinched, body got stiff. Softness with which she has been talking to him, vanished in a moment.

"Don't you think of the entire world. Put your heart in your studies. Score well. Next year you and I stay together, promise."

Prem Prakash doesn't like her to be dependent – anyone else deciding for her... but she can't help it. The more she examines herself she finds she has as much thirst for love as she has self-esteem and feeling for independence. She is a cypher without Prem Prakash. He not there and the very fire to get going, be something is extinguished; she falls deeper and deeper into despondency. Thanks to him, she learnt travelling in the train, living alone in a new city... and even now whenever she thinks of doing something, energy comes from him. He not there, she will just return to lie down here like a corpse. She is contemplating return for Siddhartha... or is it really because there is no Prem Prakash for her over there. She may not get to live with him here, but the sheer feeling that he is around, she can reach him in minutes...

Why does she feel that she can't stay in a new city for long. She is not made like Pramila who cares two hoots for the like of Rita or Principal mam, lives her own life, putting aside their taunts, searching queries. She lacks self-confidence to save herself from the hungry wolves, roaming outside. She needs a man to protect her. She needs Siddhartha too. Means that she needs this very home, or this home transported there... because if Siddhartha is there, the man living with them could only be his father. Then what's the difference, here or there?

Only the in-laws won't be there, two old guys, with whom she doesn't have much of a problem.

She doesn't have it in her to take decisions about her life without man's help. Of course, that man is one and one only – Prem Prakash. Decision to leave this city was taken with him. Without him she can do only one thing – linger on. So weak... helpless... how did she become like this or was so by birth itself?

She has come here on leave, can meet him only once. So she asked for a private meeting. Told him more about her son than about herself. Prem Prakash could see that she can't live without her son. Indian families insist on progeny, birth of a child soon after marriage, so as to keep women in life-long imprisonment. Handicap at the very outset! He felt slight contempt for her – no ambition, lacks the fire to push ahead, cutting and burning the dry bushes of handicaps and own weaknesses.

"If son's future to shape which I had gone is in jeopardy then what's the use?" She was saying.

"You didn't go out for that. You got out because you were ordered to do so. You had self-esteem, couldn't swallow that insult."

"If I come back, I would fall in your estimate... I know."

"What difference would it make?"

"Not to you... but to me. But what to do? I can't leave my son. Can leave him only under one circumstance – if you, leaving your family, start living with me."

Prem Prakash got an electric shock!

Everything around him appeared to be shaking as if in an earthquake. It took him some time to regain self-control. The girl has passed through such big calamities... yet she dreams. Her eyes were fixed at Prem Prakash, so as to catch dark, dim or bright – whatever colours appeared on Prem Prakash's face, to find out her answer in them.

Very strange... this girl. Seeking a reason outside for coming back which defaces her in her own esteem! Doesn't want to take the responsibility on herself, wants to dump it on that reason. She is romantic... but this business-like approach – 'you leave this, I leave that?' May be it happens at the peak of love when you are almost blind. Decisions about life or relationships, however, can't be taken like this, because there only that which you can do yourself lies with you, what other or others will... doesn't.

Prem Prakash's face had darkened, as if weariness of the entire world had descended there, his body turning cold, as that of a corpse.

"You know, I love you. You say truthfully – don't you?" She said.

"I do."

"Then if I am prepared to leave my son, why can't you leave your family?"

"Anna Karina had left her son behind... what happened?"

"Again Anna... book again?"

"Love is not selfish. It is in giving, not in taking."

"So far, you have only given in life; you should also learn to take."

A girl born yesterday only! Can't manage her own life, is teaching me. No, it's the new found value of the present generation – your own interest... only yours! She is saying it, but she doesn't know that she will never be able to separate herself from her child... not even when she gets to live with a man of her choice. Soon thereafter, the craving would emerge.

"You have gone there to start your new life, can find out some one compatible to you."

"And go on doing it all your life – one after another... is it? Am I a prostitute? When I have got one of my choice, why he alone should not be the first and the last? If not him, none else."

"There is big difference in your age and mine."

"It is for others, not for us if we don't feel it. Tell me—you would be healthy for next twenty years, in course of which I shall reach your level. Where the difference then?"

"What is prohibited in public should not be made public, just as kisses in public are prohibited, so we don't do it. We do it in private. Any stranger youth calls me 'uncle'. People would laugh when they will see us as... I have prestige in the society."

"Risk to your prestige... that is it. Is it not?"

A taint of taunt was on her face.

"Yes."

How similar they are on this point, he and my husband. Both bound by prestige. Husband's prestige is so hollow – I have seen. This gentleman's I have not seen but it may be equally so.

"Ok. now, what I was going to ask – if I returned and started living in the same house as before, you will close your doors to me."

"Why... I have always advocated freedom… means to live as per your convictions. You are free to decide whatever about your life. If you are unable to carry on with your husband, you are free to go with anyone else. In the same vein you also have the freedom to come back, give another trial to your earlier life, or adopt it for good. People do that – forward, backward, again forward. That's life."

Husband said – 'get out', I came out. Now he thinks that I am going very far. I do wish it – go far, very far really... but where can I go without any support? I keep slipping on the sand. Wife or

beloved? I couldn't be either. Got a husband – cruel, despot, without love; a lover bound by his prestige. He would help me from a distance. I can trust him, can live with his help and my earnings if I leave my home. He might continue meeting too. He is satisfied by helping me with money and his counsel; doesn't understand the basic—that I also need love which I didn't get so far. I can't take monetary or any help from him, if there is no love to back it. He regards me as his own, so I take his help... else do I need alms? This kind of relation – always in the air! whereas, this house – social prestige is there, if nothing else. Stamp of a wedded wife... security. Single outside... the chronic question – why not in husband's home – with which woman's right to freedom is forfeited eternally. Besides any male treats you as something 'easily available...' just because you live alone.

Whatever he might say now, husband's standing stance is – inflict torture, prick with constant taunts... tear apart, inch-by-inch. He comes flashing the sword of his 'might', husband's right! Resist... oppose... that's all which gathers in her heart for him. Standing stance of her lover is – soothing ointment on the wounds, compassion, self-less help. I want to give him the 'right'. He doesn't take it, instead hands over 'freedom' to me. I want to build a nest which has his fragrance and my stamp... where I am with him all the time, wrapped in his fragrance. He is capable... why can't he build such a nest?... because of a social bond, he has only carried as a load, his wife! Still doing it for fear of the society. He says – don't dream. Something which society can't give, will it not permit even to dream about it? Brethren! let me dream at least!

So learned and intelligent, yet the fellow doesn't understand me. So soft inside, yet at times he gets cruel. What is this – you planted a sapling... and now throwing dust on it... not letting it grow. I get caught in the whirlpool of anger for him, but strangely once out of it I am thrown back to him only.

I wished to get out of the well of this house, got out too but only to get involved with one who can't take me anywhere.

He talks about the love of heart – love which continues to flicker from afar, inspiring us to live, work, move ahead. Says love is only giving, not taking, but I want to take. I want him in flesh and blood, his touch, which I could feel in my skin, my nerves for hours, days, months, always. Then only it would reach the heart. Love in its totality, no forbiddance in matters of body, time or living together. Otherwise, what's the difference! With the husband there is body, no heart; over here there is heart, no body. Both cripple you.

This half-love is love nevertheless. That's why, despite disappointments, it gives peace and light. With the husband there is only the naked-body, dirt. In lover's love, respect for you is inherent, respect for my freedom. He may not accept me as I wish it, gives respect nonetheless... else what is in me that could inspire love or respect? I am nothing before him; his magnitude that he gives respect to me, a particle of dust otherwise, whose very existence husband seeks to rub out.

My fate that I was to get only half. Had the full been my destiny, I would have taken birth in a complete family, where husband and wife lived together. I was pushed all the time – from mother to stepmother, from her to in-laws... incomplete

there too. I could also have been given a gentleman in the husband!

Half-lover that my lover is... I should take it as my destiny and be satisfied. What's wrong if days pass like this only... 'Desires know no bounds.'

This itself is enough that a chap gives me respect, love, fills me with light... which help me to save myself while living with a monster.

But dependent – physically or mentally – now I won't be, not even of my lover. No help in my career or struggle which henceforth shall be on my own strength. Prem Prakash also desired to see me in this mould. Now it will be on equal terms with him. If we get love, we give it; we give it so we get it. I will now take my own decisions, without consulting anyone. Will shape my future myself.

While returning, she was thinking all the time about it during her rail-journey. The way she is made, two things are primary: (1) Difficult for her to stay alone outside home. She lacks strength to face the society, all by herself; breaks down easily (2) she has distaste for men from the very beginning... so far she could like only two – her father and Prem Prakash.

It is security that she needs from man – that wolves do not attack. At best, she needs a man for those errands where woman alone can't manage. The difficulty is that any man who happens to give a helping hand even in small matters, immediately starts asking for biggish things in return. Is it possible that she asks her husband to provide only two things (1) security of home and for this he has not to take any trouble, it would come automatically. (2) Coming forward sometimes to help in such matters where man is required. In return, she would take care of the household, cook for everyone, look after the son. Their relationship should be with the home and not with each other. Both stay within limits. Her objective is son's education, his overall development. For his sake she would compromise with the young guru, putting aside her ego. Current year of the boy is gone, full care about his studies has to be taken next year and she alone has to do it because none else in the family is interested in it.

That which she wants for herself, she would also give – freedom. She would let him think it over thoroughly. In a week she conveyed her conditions to him –

(1) Wherever she is next year onwards, Siddhartha shall stay with her. She would live where her job is. Can also return if she gets a job there, else would bring Siddhartha here.

(2) They could stay under the same roof as guardians of Siddhartha, husband and wife for appearances' sake only. No physical between them. She would do the domestic chores beyond service-hours to the extent time and her energy permit.

(3) She would spend her entire earnings on Siddhartha and herself. Would not ask him or family a penny, nor give them any

(4) Both shall be independent in their lives. Young guru takes up a job or not, any occupation or not will be his concern. They won't interfere in each other's matters. The same thing shall apply about meeting people. They shall not force each other to meet or not meet a particular individual. However, in her movements, she would take due care about her marital status and prestige of the house.

(5) Sex between them – on which the young guru lays so much emphasis – is possible but for that just being a married couple won't suffice. Bondage of heart is essential. So, it will depend on their future conduct, shall not be claimed as a matter of right by either.

Clear-cut conditions from her side, about things which were bones of contention between them. Young guru agreed promptly. His concealed goals were being achieved – wife should not settle down there; she living here, prestige would automatically come. She will take on herself all domestic responsibilities, young guru having freedom and plenty of time to meet Nisha whenever he, likes. Showing extra enthusiasm he said –

"Then should I start searching a job for you here?"

She laughed within her sleeves – fellow can't find out a job for himself, shall get it for others? Will do it on what strength – guru's throne-like seat? She, however, said something else –

"If I can take anyone's help for it, why not yours! But you shall not put me under any obligation later on, nor would ask me in exchange to do anything in particular... I know you do it."

"No no... let everyone try – me, you, Prem Prakash Sir too. Owner of 'Nagar bandhu' newspaper has opened a school. He is my devotee. If you agree, I give him your bio-data."

"I have no objection but you will please remember what I just now said about obligation, also the terms we agreed upon."

"Of course... of course."

Young guru's laugh was a hollow one.

Not on Prem Prakash's, nor Guru's but on her own strength, she got a job this time – in the hometown, not in Nagar bandhu's school, in another. The school where she taught in the new city was so prestigious that experience of it made all the difference.

On coming back, however she fell into remorse – with great difficulty she had got a chance of moving out from here; was just settling down in the new city that she again threw herself back into the same muck. Weakness for the son... but she could have taken him there, could have got him admitted in some school there – may not be of high grade? Had she tried she could also have got him admitted in her school itself. Boy's education – was it only a pretext to come back? She wanted the fore-walls of home, security of the husband. Stepping out for each little thing of setting up the household, to be stared at in the process – all around greedy eyes of young and the old... as if row of ants creeping over your body! She couldn't face all this, ran away.

She didn't have the courage to meet Prem Prakash. Thread between them – she having the desire... drive to move up and Prem Prakash helping – had broken. For him she must have fallen from grace. With what face now would she go to him... and for what? Is his assistance required in matters which lie between herself and her husband? What can he do there? She has to do, whatever is to be done.

If she has fallen from grace for Prem Prakash he too is no longer the same for her. Did he do what should have been done for the sake of love which developed between them, which both regard precious? He seeks love which doesn't disturb in the least the world he has created for himself. That world intact, the upper floor can have whatever... even something spicy to add flavour to life. The moment his world appears threatened, he moves back – cowardice! She won't go to him now. If he takes care of his home she would take care of hers. Siddhartha gaining in confidence was in the meanwhile a matter of satisfaction for her.

Not just in the wake of the recent compromise between them, she had been indifferent towards the activities of her husband for quite some time. Now it was complete detachment, dry indifference. She was not concerned until some conduct of the husband affected her or her son. She didn't ask him or in-laws, for any expenditure over herself, her son – school-fee, other related expenses, e.g. dress, boy's going to school picnic, tutor's pay etc. She would also not hand over her salary or any part thereof to them as was done earlier.

She was not interested in investigating Nisha's visits, nor did she have time for the same. Sometimes news did come trickling down to her – Nisha's scooty parked outside the temple even late at night. She didn't feel pangs of jealousy, natural in a wife. Conversely she felt relieved – the more young guru is involved in Nisha, safer she is. Not that she pushed him towards Nisha, she was simply unconcerned... an attitude which earlier existed in a seed-form, had sprouted and had now taken shape... because there was thought behind it; she had reached here only gradually. So, even when she learnt that the young-guru had purchased a bike for Nisha, she didn't feel anything. She was happy that she was now totally unconcerned about anything of the young-guru. She expected the same in him on matters related to her.

Unfortunately it didn't last long. Distance – from young guru so that he doesn't figure in her thinking at all – couldn't be secured. Barely three months had passed that young guru appeared to be switching back. Now sometimes, in passing, he would touch her shoulder or feigning to draw her attention to something would draw her by the arm towards himself... all the while pretending casual. Might be... but she felt as earlier – a lizard creeping over... so nauseating! She, however, continued to ignore. After all they lived under the same roof, were husband and wife... may be only for appearances sake; distance which she desired was hardly possible. But soon murmurings followed – "You don't ever sit with me, you just put meals formally on the table, never dine with me, no time to talk to me!" In reality she was always short of time. Six hours in the school, two hours to and fro, mass of school work to be done at home like copy correction etc., over and above domestic work she had taken upon herself; on Sundays and holidays – washing and pressing her and Siddhartha's clothes, preparing for the week ahead... where was the time? On the other hand for young guru it was loitering at home whole day long. On return from the school, she desired that no one should talk to her and vice versa; she was dead tired speaking all the while in the school, wished that she may not have to speak at all at home... while here was the young guru – whole day at home, no work, eager for conversation. If not she, the son, at least, should talk... tell him what passed off in his school today. But the boy too imitating his mother, gave him the go bye, leaving young guru starved. She realized his plight but bitterly thought that the solution lay in his hands only – why he doesn't go out to work! One holiday, however, the young guru in desperation did detain her – "Do I not deserve even a couple of minutes of yours?" – he asked point-blank.

"Why not! We do talk about household affairs. Nothing ever stops. Ok, tell me, what do you want to say."

"We talk only about material things, never anything else."

She didn't say anything. Young guru should remember all that has passed between them, also the compromise they reached before her return. The trouble is that he very easily forgets whatever is unpalatable for him, whereas she can't forget a thing, even details linger on.

"Am I nothing to you?"

"Why not. We live together, have been doing for so many years; we look after each other in sickness. You are father of my son whom I am educating. I cook for you and your parents. If any maid doesn't turn up, I do her work... all this because you are what you are of mine."

"That which is between husband and wife... is it there?"

"That alone is not what matters. You probably have forgotten what we had decided. It was only after you agreed that I returned."

"I thought you would reform with time."

"The same language again!" – She lost temper – "Who are you to reform me. First reform yourself."

"How have I to... tell me. I will do your bidding."

"The same again! I don't want to get into arguments – as we did earlier. You think about what you have to do... it's none of my concerns. You attend to your things, I to mine..."

And she got up.

Things bygone have come to the fore again. So many feuds, fights... and we have not moved an inch. The clock of this man's life is stuck up at a point, where alone it rotates, creating whirling sound. Not much of a change in me either – moved a step forward only to take two backwards... threw myself back into the same mess, to get out of which was once a matter of life and death. Prem Prakash sir was with me then. Now I don't simply have the courage to meet him and he – of course, he knows that I have returned – never phoned on his own, shows that he is hurt. Who knows he has stepped aside to let me improve with husband, my conjugal life. He is like that only.

Home... is as it was, shall remain the same. Relation with husband may improve probably... but I myself am not keen. Sometimes, I pity this man – what do I give him in return while he keeps me in his house. I have distaste for the body whereas he is all urge, is young. But I can't help it. Whenever I try to discover something good in him, I hit upon his fluffy lips, small hair, red attire and above all crooked smile of a villain... combined they generate nausea. I feel the moment his lips touched me anywhere, I may not be able to control the vomit which might straight be thrown on his face. Only way to give myself to him is what I did earlier – just lie down under him like a machine, eyes fixed on

the ceiling, let him do his liking and wait for the moment when he is done and the dirty act is over. Means, here too it would be the same as before. Not just one night, he would then crush me every night. Squeezed in the school, do I have stamina enough to be squeezed again at home? He, a bull, idling whole day long at home.

You are a woman – anyone would say – you have to save the home, protect and shape it. Keeping that end in view have to reform this man. He keeps asking – what should he do to have me, but can it be such business – "I do this, so now you do that?" Alright then what really should he do that I come to tolerate him at least. He should leave this temple business, take up some job, earn, hand over money, fulfill our requirements, become responsible. Then something is possible. His image may improve gradually. The fellow, however, wants immediate returns. The very first day he would go to the office, he will come to demand – "attended office on your bidding, now give...." Time for something to grow inside, matters of heart, etc. he just can't imagine. For him, female is only a body, no heart there, as he doesn't have one.

The aspersions this man threw at me in the presence of his parents, the way he dragged me on the staircase shouting—'get out'... can all that be forgotten simply because I returned? Was it only a routine skirmish between husband and wife?

No, it's not simply a reaction, it is her subconscious.

She commenced doing some errands of young guru – arranging sheets on his side of the bed in the morning, as she did hers. Sometimes washing his shirt-pants along with Siddhartha's and her clothes, press them... but his red attire never. Just sitting before him while he ate was not possible... but she tried to dine with him along with Siddhartha as is the vogue in other families. Sometimes she even waited for him to come for dinner; if he was in the temple, would send a word through Siddhartha.

Some possibility there... of course, if the young guru changes. If he does on her or anyone else's asking, the change won't be a real one, only outward. Real change can come about, if something indeed grows inside him... so intense that he can't live without changing. Of course, someone from outside may also implant—as Prem Prakash Sir did in my case. However, I can't have that influence over him because I don't have that delicate touch which Prem Prakash Sir had for me. Nisha might have.

On return, her behaviour with Nisha, as with young guru had been quite formal. She now commenced infusing a little delicacy there. Stopped criticising the young guru, restrained herself even when provoked. It might bring about some change in the young guru and, subsequently, in her too.

She was trying... that suddenly one night there was an uproar. Siddhartha and she had gone to sleep, the young guru having not come. Quite often, he came late from the temple. By then, these two would retire for the night because they had to get up early in the morning. When young guru came later, he would dine alone and later quietly slip into the bed on Siddhartha's side. He was in no hurry to get up early in the morning.

Father-in-law was waking her up in panic.

"Bhaiya has locked himself in the temple. We knocked and knocked, he is not opening... may do something untoward, come down at once."

It was past midnight. Young guru was never so late. She ran downstairs, following her father in-law. The inner room of the temple was bolted from inside. In-laws, and a couple of neighbours were beating the door, calling the young guru from outside. There was however, no trace of any sound inside. Beating of the door in the quietness of midnight sounded all the more loudly, hearing which a few other neighbours also arrived.

After awhile, a neighbour suggested – "we shouldn't delay, let us break open." And without waiting for any response he rushed to his home next door, brought an axe and started breaking the door with it. More people had gathered in the meanwhile.

"Take care, the broken door may fall upon him." Someone from the crowd counselled. There upon the hitter, giving up the idea of breaking the door proceeded to create a hole in it downwards. Hole created, he peeped inside – young guru lying on the floor was looking at the hole... eyes wide open.

"Guruji, Guruji... are you ok? Please open the door."

Young guru in the same posture kept looking... didn't utter a word, didn't open the door either. The same situation persisting even after repeated requests, the man with the axe started widening the hole. Now small sounds emanated from inside, followed by slightly bigger ones – of opening and closing of the iron-almirah. The man with the axe again peeped inside and whispered to the gathering – 'has got up.'

"Guruji, please open the door. We are worried about you. Else the door will have to be broken unnecessarily."

After awhile the door opened. Young guru in his red attire – face and eyes equally red – closing the door behind him, bypassing Devi's throne, moved in small steps, towards the area outside, in the open. Those who had gathered followed him. Taking a few more steps ahead in the open, he suddenly took an about turn and started rather loudly –

"This is Satyendra speaking. (Satyendra, his parents' adopted son, who had committed suicide). The woman in the house has illicit relationship with another man. You can't see, but I who am in the sky can see all. You don't see me, even when I am around. I am everywhere. I see all...

"Baré's voice! His soul is wandering. God... it has entered Bhaiya..."

It was young guru's father... almost crying. Hearing about soul wandering, people moved aside, trying to keep safe distance from the young guru. They were now slightly scared of him.

The young guru, treading like an angel, was now addressing the gathering before him –

"Throw her out immediately, that lady of bad morals... else this house... colony shall be ruined. Ruin! Three years elapsed and she has not established any physical relationship with her husband because she has it with an outsider. Turn her out. If you seek your safety, get her out immediately."

She, stuck at the door, was looking, hearing too. Standing above in the balcony of her room was Siddhartha, who had been awakened by the noise outside. When the young guru raising his voice repeated twice or thrice that she should be turned out, she ran inside... the same house from where the young guru a year earlier had asked her to get out. What he had said then inside the house before family members, he was now shouting outside... before the public.

How insulting! To face abuses, physical torture inside the house was nothing compared to this. The guy, casting slur on his wife in public is, in turn, throwing mud on himself... but who knows it is really his brother ghost speaking, voice appears to be slightly different.

That point... where you are completely helpless. Leaving everything to the circumstances, the world or God, you just run away to take refuge under whatever is available then. If nothing else, then your body's cage... hide yourself under its cover. Whatever happening, let it, because you just don't have any control over it.

She tried to move away from the noise outside as far as was possible. People who had gathered also slipped away, amused, after pushing the young guru and his parents into their house. Father left the young guru temporarily with his mother to go and lock the temple from outside.

She was in her room with her son, who, having watched the drama was still scared. The door of the house had been closed, but all was not quiet in the drawing room below. Young guru's parents were busy cajoling him, pouring cold water on his head, making him suck tulsi-leaves and curd but Satyendra inside the young guru was still on –

"Out... woman of bad morals out. I will not leave, stay here in this body only, until thou art gone."

"Brother... where to send her" – father of young guru implored. "The house we lived earlier has been sold out. The girl has no relatives... Where will she go..." He folded his hands.

"Go anywhere... but get out, only then I will leave this house, this body."

The more the father implored, the more his son – adopted or real, dead or alive – shouted –

"Nothing! She has been given much freedom which has spoiled her. She... throw her out right now."

"At this hour of the night?"

"There is no night or day where I am. A woman of bad morals can't stay near the temple, in the house of religious leanings.

Get her out... now, this moment."

Father-in-law, scared, almost crying ran to her upstairs.

"Baré's soul is in a rebellious mood, is insistent. You go somewhere now, come back in the morning. Baré's soul will leave Bhaiya's body, once you left. You go just now... anywhere. If anything happens to Bhiaya, I am finished."

Without saying a word, she took out the bag from the almirah, put clothes she had to wear for the school tomorrow, Siddhartha's over them. Took all the money she had, Siddhartha by his arm and went down the stairs. In the drawing room, young guru sat with his mother. She didn't look at them. Siddhartha, of course, kept looking back at his father. Poor boy was still terribly scared.

Out... in the open. It was all quiet... where a little while ago there was so much of hustle. She won't get a three wheeler anywhere nearby at this odd hour. Spending the remainder of the night in a park... was dangerous, she being a woman. She took out her scooty, seated Siddhartha behind her and moved out. If nowhere, platform of the station could be her shelter... but bathroom?

Father-in-law has advised her to come back in the morning. She could while away time anywhere till dawn and then go back... to the same house from where she is turned out again and again. School – she has to go, Siddhartha too. Throw yourself into work... that alone can wash out the bad dream of the night. Wash it out of your mind, Siddhartha's as well. It was worthwhile that both stay away, until coming back from their schools.

She checked in a hotel nearby. In the morning, both took their respective school buses, putting the scooty in the parking joint.

Back in the afternoon. Same house from where she is turned out in varied ways, turns back too in diverse ways.

Everything was like any other day as if nothing had happened last night. Young guru was fast asleep in the upper room as usual. There was food on the table for her and Siddhartha. Remainder of what mother in-law had cooked for the young guru. Both changed, took meals and sat down with their work as they did every day – Siddhartha his homework, she copy-correction. The afternoon siesta was the good fortune of the like of young guru who had no work, who stayed home day in and day out.

Five in the evening young guru got up... almost in time when she prepared coffee. She took it upstairs for the young guru too, milk for Siddhartha, as always.

No one spoke till Siddhartha was upstairs; when he went out to play, the young guru harped on his pet theme –

"On return from the school, you sit down with school copies. Not a word with me... as if I am not at home."

"Have you left me with any face to do it?"

"You would say the same – that I don't go out on job, lie down in this house whole day... ok... say that only."

"That's obvious. What is not, you make it so by talking all sort of rubbish before all and sundry. Earlier whatever you said you did inside the house, now you do it outside. Did you not feel ashamed to parade yourself and your wife naked before public?"

Anger burst out at last. Young guru's face was taut in surprise.

"What did I say... and to whom... when?"

"Last midnight only, in the temple, outside in the open, before everyone. Where was the necessity of playing all that drama?"

"Last midnight?... I was fast asleep throughout. Rather overslept – got up only now. No idea when both of you left for the school."

"Your religion, worshippings... do they also teach you to tell lies, one after the other? You know very well what you said before the public out in the open there... cast aspersions on me before all and sundry, said that I have illicit relations with another person. This indirectly indicts you too – you didn't bother. Turned me out at night; I stayed in a hotel with Siddhartha. Had I the money, I would have continued there only, never returned."

"I am positive – I didn't say anything to anyone last night. I didn't meet anyone. I was asleep. Slept first on deewan down below and later on this cot here."

"Whoop... what innocence! Go and check with those who gave you birth... the mischief you played last night, see the room in the temple, the door which had to be broken with an axe. You left no stone unturned to mire my image or Siddhartha's. You had none anyway. Even after all this you expect that any woman worth the salt will let you touch her. If she does you will go and announce in public through a similar drama – "Lo and behold – now she has started sleeping with me."

Young guru couldn't take it anymore. Picked up the towel and slipped into the bathroom.

Young guru had taken ill.

She got the doctor to examine him, was found suffering from gastic trouble and acidity. Liver slightly affected. She purchased the medicines, gave him while at home, briefed him properly when away. Cooked the food advised for him; in the evenings served it herself. All this she did with a feeling of detachment as if home was a hospital, young guru a patient and she a nurse. You shouldn't have any ill feeling for the sick and who knows – departed soul might indeed have entered his body, shook it badly.

She had to go to Doctor's clinic for further advice. His fee... more medicines which will have to be bought... she asked mother-in-law to give her the money required as she didn't have enough.

"Get it from his purse which would be in the almirah at the temple."

Mother in-law handed over a bunch of keys, identifying three – of the outside gate of the temple, of the inner room, and the almirah.

The door, which had been holed... had since been repaired... a wooden piece having been fixed there.

She was entering this room only a second time. First time when she was shown – the room which young guru got it done for himself specially. It was simply glamorous then; now she was enveloped by foul smell the moment she entered. She felt choked... as if someone was putting a noose round her neck with a dirty saari. She got scared for a moment... the ghost might be hiding here... and she is enemy number one. She instantly stepped out, the clean air refreshed her. She stood at the doorstep for a while, leaving the doors open. The room closed for all these days, foul smell gathered... she should think, rationally, not succumb to blind faith, believing in ghosts, etc.

The foul smell thinned out but didn't go altogether. Not her concern anyway, she has not to be here. Just open the almirah, take out the purse, lock and move out. She covered her nose with her dupatta and headed straight to the almirah. The moment it opened, she, as it were got a slap of the foul smell on her face. The almirah contained bottles of Vodka, Rum, country liquor – full, half, empty, quite a few left open....

There were also glasses unwashed... a few having remnants of liquor at the bottom.

The man who had taken deeksha, Swami with the red robe, guru, devotee, preacher, reformer... Shree Shree108 Shree Swami... Anand, master-astrologer!

'Hypocrite!'... she sometimes abuses him, but he really turned out to be one. Who knows, they might also be eating fish-meat here just next to the temple. Plates were there... albeit clean and arranged on one side.

She took out the purse, closed the almirah with a big push and quickly walked out. Dutifully locked the almirah, room and the temple. Handing over the keys and the purse to mother-in-law, she said –

"Give two hundred bucks to me and if you so like, go and see in his almirah the deities your son keeps and worships."

Not responding, the mother in-law mechanically gave her the money and went inside the kitchen – as if nothing was said or heard.

She didn't say anything to the young guru. They didn't have the relationship to question each other in their realms. Of course, compassion which was gradually descending upon her for of a sick person disappeared, only formality remained.

She didn't mention it to anyone else either. However, the issue once came up casually with Nisha, when they were alone. Lately, she had started treating her with a little affection and respect.

"Do you know that your guru ji drinks."

"Sometimes he does – he told me" – Nisha replied with such abandon that she was taken aghast. Probably Nisha had not seen the heap of bottles in the almirah.

"You never stopped him?"

"He knows better, his concern. He never drank before me, nor I ever found him drunk. He didn't conceal it either. Every second man drinks these days."

In terms of years, Nisha was only slightly junior but clearly she belonged to the new generation.

"You have no difficulty with him over this?"

"How me..." She shrugged her shoulders. "It's his business..."

"You should have forbidden him..."

"Why should I get into all this? You deal with it... both of you."

Nisha very clearly dissociated herself. The bad company which drinks would bring to the young guru or the adverse effect it would have on his health was none of her concerns. Everyone in the house knew that Nisha was close to him but neither Nisha directly or in-laws through Nisha ever cautioned the young guru. Surprisingly they didn't feel even the pinch. It was she who felt it – although they had separated... almost. Is it because she is still his wife after all. Associations of a wife! Yes... that is why, she had set upon the course of reforming him, was executing it honestly till the drama at the temple. Even thereafter, sometimes she came to half believing – the departed soul might indeed have entered his body! The curtains were finally drawn when she saw in his room – bottles, glasses, plates. God knows for how long has all this been going on. Sure enough, that night the young guru was drunk, playing drama of the departed soul.

She felt dejected. Things which have not to improve, do not – whatever you do.

There was a time when she could go to any limits doing the biddings of this man. Took 'deeksha' as desired by him, participated in religious rituals with equal enthusiasm – if he organised 'langar', she cooked for about three hundred people, was in the kitchen since morning till late at night. Danced with other women during festivals... sometimes till sores appeared on the feet. Distaste set in when she saw that this man was devoid of any compassion, which is the essence of religion. He was engaged only in show-off, parading the external. That religion should change your inner-self did not occur to him.

Strangely her life takes two steps forward only to move two and a half backwards. Prem Prakash Sir used to say – it happens in life – going forward, return, forward again. But funnily in her case 'the return' lands her precisely at the point she proceeded from. Presently she finds herself at the same point – where she was, she too, the same – no change. No effect visible on her of the few steps forward she took. No trace of them! Life which got stuck at this door-step simply refuses to move.

Her mistake. She got a chance, she should have fully utilized it. She had only to keep going straight. If it couldn't be done, she should have at least kept away from this place. Swayed away midway to dump herself here again. Insecurity, diffidence probably. Cover of a camouflage – that she was returning for the sake for her son.

Now helplessly, she looks at the shocks being inflicted on the poor boy, one after the other. The sight of a drunk father every second day, dramas he enacts, mother being paraded/naked in public by father only, not bothering that his son is also present there. What image of his parents is being imprinted on the poor soul, his adolescent mind – drunkard father, adulterous mother! Had she visualised all this, she would have never come back.

Now from here? When she would get another chance again, if at all, to run away. Thoroughly dejected, exhausted, she is stuck in this house like a machine crackling at a joint. From here to school, back again. School work, house work, again school work. No place where she can go even for a small change. Not yet old but already tired of living. Months pass by and not a single occasion when she would have had even a small laugh. No direction in life, no hope. No enthusiasm left for anything. Life, it seems, takes a leap only once, somewhere when you are between twenty five and thirty; if unavailed, remaining years it simply crawls, like an earthen worm on a muddy floor!

Those with no zeal... they also live after all and she was also doing it – that Prem Prakash came and lit the fire of life in her. Hope, enthusiasm, speed, dreams – all sprouted one by one, only to vanish so soon and she left in a starless night... desolate, darker than what it was before. Prem Prakash dropped out somewhere on the way... but it was she who had decided that, henceforth, she alone would deal with her life, would not take refuge in him, whatever comes. She stopped phoning him. He had also advocated that she should be self-reliant.

Now nothing is going to happen. She would lie here only, buried like a machine, growling underground. Five-six years hence, Siddhartha would grow up, capable of thinking about himself and she would be touching thirty-five-forty. Life over.

So many lives pass away like this... finished midway!

She wants to come... again.

Again she would open the gate, as she did when she came for the first time – to invite me for her college. What resonance was there in her voice then, what zeal? Today it was a voice defeated... tired.

What have I done to her! Yes, I am responsible. She was raw; it was I who was led away with feelings, made her flow along. Only this time when she returned and I felt she was busy reshaping her life, I kept away trying to rise above attachment. It has however come again, it always does... she is coming.

Whosoever this girl leaned upon... slipped away one by one – mother, father, brother, husband. And now me too.

Her mother – a lover. Fell in love with a married man, who appeared from nowhere, gave herself to

him selflessly. Kept with herself till alive the children she got from him... so that no disturbance is caused to his family-life.

Her father – also a lover. Admitted love. After the death of his beloved, brought home the flowers of their love, risking family-feud. He also, till alive, gave the children upbringing, love too.

Where did they go wrong – these two? Both observed what can be called morality of love. Now a child of these two lovers... if she doesn't have thirst for love, who else will...?

Her brother... in the absence of parents, kept a circle of security around his sister. He too...

These three come to me from the world of the dead...

A woman of wheatish complexion, physically sumptuous. Big nose-ring, equally big earings. Her mid hair-line decorated with a biggish silver chain with one end having half moon-shaped round silver plate on it hanging on the forehead. The plate lightly swings around, causing the silver chain to slip away from the hair-line. She is rubbing the black utensils of her kitchen with ash. Smoke arising from the tents of nomads' dwelling. About hundred yards away, her two children are playing – there, a small girl with very smooth arms. The woman calls her son playing little further away from his sister – "Chandu, my boy! Take care of chunmun..." That sound reaches me. I hear it.

A man dead – body wrapped in a white sheet laid on the floor, cotton on his nostrils – suddenly gets up, putting aside the sheet. Declining age, soft face of sweet demeanour, small round drop of white tilak on the forehead, smallish hair on the head... entire being soaked in sweetness...

Getting into his cotton shoes, he goes out – 'Chandu'... where are you? I had taken great care of myself for the sake of you two... now you take care of your younger sister. Where are you, my son... where is your bicycle?

My eyes look for the bicycle.

A lean and thin lad in pyjama-shirt-chappal surrounded by flames, trying to pierce them and come out – "Papa! I had heard your voice, coming... I want to live... I am coming...."

White pyjama and shirt, in flames... now a mass of fire coming towards me. Had he been alive, today he would be only slightly younger to me.

To my wife, I am only a husband... but to this girl I am mother, father and brother too... all rolled into what can be called a lover. There won't be much difference to my wife's life whether I live or not – may be some little temporary grief, luxury of the rich, but she would live on, as before – whereas it would be a matter of life and death for this girl. She can go the way her father, mother and brother have gone.

What she should have got anyway, she didn't get – mother, brother, nor a husband of normal attributes. Little comfort of these she gets from me and that puts life into her. Should I care for those sticking to my circle, or this girl... the little chunmun? Chunmun of a father full of sweetness, chunmun who didn't have childhood or youth... future also dark.

But thirst for love... which she has... was it quenched in any case, anytime, that it does in her case? Sooner or later she will have to climb down to the dull pattern of life... whether she goes with me or anyone else. Love, after all, is a leap in the air. For how long can one hang there!

If the being of this girl is love and love alone, it may not necessarily be so in my case. I may be of the tribe of a spider – weaving a net for itself, up and down on it. Both have the right to recognize and follow their respective natures. No, not a matter of right, they shall do only that. If she fails to shape me in her image, she is dejected, whereas I happen to be treading only my path, simultaneously loving her too.

She is ignorant. Lets herself flow, doesn't hold herself. She has to learn it, if she has to survive. Will she learn from me? No, only life would teach her... onslaughts of life would, while I am all the time trying to shield her from the onslaughts. I give love – my type – so that she survives at least.

But for how long can we go trying—I to save her and she to save herself through me. Will I ever be able to give any direction to her life?

And all this – to save and be saved, giving direction, etc., all this... is it not just deluding ourselves?

Mystery... that life gives us the kick under illusions... only to come out all of sudden and tear them off into pieces. We don't see life as such, but we do see whatever happens consequentially. That's what is called destiny.

To live our illusions to the point of destiny appearing – that's all which probably we can do. Thereafter to carry the load of our respective destinies...

Downpour. After narrating all that had happened till date since her coming, she said—"I thought now my battle I will fight... won't trouble you... but what can I do if I can't manage without you. I feel, coming back was a big mistake, it turned out to be snake-ladders game. I landed at snake's mouth, tried to improve matters, which only got worse.

"Everything is not always in our hands."

"Living away from you. I tried that too."

"Now what do you think?"

"I can't, could you think?"

"Regarding what?"

"Regarding yourself, myself."

"You were right when you said that I never thought about myself. Always gave priority to giving rather than snatching something for myself. I am made that way only. That nature brought me close to you and the same dictates that I can never leave my wife. You can earn, she doesn't know even how to draw money from the bank. If I can come forward to help you, how can I leave her helpless?"

"You don't love her."

"It may not be love, but we have lived together for years. She may be nothing but is co-traveller nonetheless. To leave co traveller midway...?

Then the point where I am today... by the time one reaches there, life has already woven a net around you. This net alone becomes your identity. The net in my case is – the position I hold, reputation in the society... me such and such person etc. This net has been carved out by various strings. If I tear it off, I loose my identity itself."

"It is identity in society... there is something like self-identity – of your inner-being."

"You can say that but an ordinary person lives clinging only to the identity which is his in the society."

"You are not an ordinary person."

"Everyone is ordinary at the level of living life. I can't bring completeness to your life. Probably, no one can, because your son won't accept anyone and you won't leave him, whatever you say. If you do under some provocation, you would always remain a divided self."

"Means our love is nothing... that which we gave each other these years? Is it simply nothing?

"No, it remains the ultimate truth... that's the whole trouble.

Life envelops it in such a way that it can't be easily identified."

"I don't understand all these big things. Straightway I want to know one thing – what are you in my life and I need to know it here and now."

She suddenly became tense, as happened with her quite often. Prem Prakash was taken aback, but he collected himself.

"You always said that I think a lot and lot thinking does not lead us anywhere. Then why not take – where life has brought us to be as that which life has thought out for us...

You want to know what I am to you in your life, then listen – I am... whatever by now life has made me out for you. I am your mother, father, brother... whosoever was snatched away from you, or you didn't get—lover too. I am all that. I am your Maayka, which you were not destined to have. Maayka, meaning the place where an Indian girl, whenever in distress, comes to take refuge, as you have come to me. She gathers courage there and then moves on. If a place can be 'maayka', why not a person?

"I can't live with you."

"May not... but support remains all the same. Living together brings in so many troubles... the crackling of utensils, you know... that sometimes the very base, the support – which is the main thing – slips away. That which would lend some meaning to your life, which has already become your life's aim in your subconscious is shaping your son's life. The incompleteness which was in your life, the slips... may not be in his. Concentrate on this. Not much adverse has befallen you. Had a fall only. Get up, collect yourself and move on. I am with you, shall always be. Now say it again—"Keep me along with you."

Tears lurking in her eyes, rolled down in a stream. Her shirt got soaked. Prem Prakash took her in his embrace.

Agitation and bitterness inside were washed away. Path beyond appeared clean and fresh... Prem Prakash too. She felt like having bathed moments before.

"Very soon I will go out on another job, this time taking my son along... and will never return to that house."

She decisively said, wiping her eyes with Prem Prakash's kurta. Prem Prakash patted her on the back.

□□□